REAPING HELLFIRE

Also By Keith Remer

Killing Bardoe, Book One of The Calamitous Breed Trilogy

Blood City, Book Two of The Calamitous Breed Trilogy

North of the Brazos

In the Midst of Wolves

Run River Run

The Aristocracy of Caddo County

The Hiding Place of Thunder

REAPING HELLFIRE

By

KEITH REMER

Honey Lee Press
Oklahoma City

Reaping Hellfire

First Honey Lee Press trade paperback edition May 2020
Manufactured in the United States of America
10 9 8 7 6 5 4 3 2 1

Print ISBN 978-1-7341015-5-3
eBook ISBN 978-1-7341015-6-0
Library of Congress Control Number: 2020906764

For a dear friend of over forty years,

David Shupe

He's been with me every step of the way.

PROLOGUE

In the course of a very long life, Stew Graybow killed more than his fair share of the Comanche, along with two white men, and one Mexican. Never did he despise any of them as much as he did the man presently sprawled at his feet.

The lawman lying on the dirt street of Beaver City took four bullets from the Apache and a crazy laughing son of a bitch before stumbling out of the saloon. Then Graybow put three more bullets in the middle of his back, and still the lawman twitched as his blood flowed from his tattered body like water from an overturned bucket.

Wooly's chest heaved as he fought for his last breaths of air. Graybow's eyes were drawn to the silver star pinned to the lapel of the lawman's vest. It moved up and down with the efforts Wooly made to stay alive. Graybow would have preferred to stand in place watching the man suffer, but town folk would soon come pouring into the streets and might harbor a desire for vengeance.

Because the man lying at his feet managed to destroy Graybow's life, the old Indian fighter raised his revolver and bent at the waist for a close-up shot. The bullet pierced the badge, and no doubt did the same to Wooly's heart, for he took not another breath.

"May you be damned to hell, Wooly," Graybow grumbled as he first tucked his pistol away and then bent to jerk the silver star from the dead man's chest.

Oklahoma Territory

And

Northeast Texas

1897

CHAPTER ONE

Lordy, Lordy

The Apache rode into the Kiowa settlement outside Fort Sill in Oklahoma Territory, sitting arrogantly erect in his silver laden saddle. The conquered remnants of a once proud nation stared enviously at his coal black stallion and the fineness of his apparel and exhibited weaponry. None blocked his way. They were of a different blood but knew well his reputation. Men who wished to do him harm most likely believed him to be in New Mexico Territory, but the "man of many names" came here as a result of a vision. He reigned to a stop before an ancient hag squatted beside a fire outside a lodge. She looked as worn from defeat as the other people of the settlement. He knew of the woman only from what white men would consider a dream, and he did not show her the respect of dismounting. The wounds he'd suffered over a year in the past from the famed lawman, CB Wooly, had yet to completely heal. He did not care to let this woman or her tribesman witness the limp in his walk.

"Do you know of me, old woman?" he called down to the revered crone before the fire, using her native language. The Apache could use her words as efficiently as he could that of the white man.

"I know you stink of death," she responded in a raspy voice tinged with both animosity and fear.

"Of those I've inflicted…or of my own?" He asked.

The old woman offered nothing more than a taunting chuckle.

"Two dead men haunt my sleep," he said after deciding to ignore her arrogance. "It's said you know the future. What does mine hold?"

The decrepit sorceress pulled a small leather pouch from her tattered deerskin robe and emptied its contents on the ground between her feet. With gnarled hands she shuffled a collection of trinkets and charms the Apache could not identify while she mumbled words too faint to recognize. The woman looked up and back into the Apache's eyes revealing a glint of satisfaction.

"You need not fear the dead in this life. It is the living that will insure your demise. Before the snow falls again, you will be no more. The dead simply await your arrival. Only then should you concern yourself with the plans they have for your torment."

The Apache pulled in a deep breath of air through his nose before smiling down upon the ancient figure. Slowly and deliberately he removed a nickel-plated Smith and Wesson .44 caliber from a bejeweled holster of silver and turquoise, and pointed it at the woman's deeply creased face.

"Do not consider this an act of brutality, but rather one of release. Go before me old woman as my special messenger. Worn those who wait that it is a most endearing alliance I hold with the devil."

The Apache put one bullet between the woman's eyes and then looked to his left and right for any that might take offense at his action. Those looking on did not flee but neither would they meet the Apache's glare. Turning his snorting stallion in place with only the pressure of a knee, the man in braids, and derby, and apparel as black as his horse, rode from the settlement sitting arrogantly erect in the saddle.

* * * *

"Grab his other leg, Tom! Get holt of that other damn leg!" the apparent ring leader bellowed.

Walker's two arms and left leg presently supported three gnarling and cursing no accounts. He'd be damned before letting the forth one grab his free leg, which he kept busy kicking at and stomping on the three holding him. Walker found hope in that the Tom feller seemed to lose interest in trying for the leg after connecting more than once with both toe and heel of Walker's well-worn military issue cavalry boots.

Walker had not yet caught the name of the man trying to control his right arm, but the one tugging on his left answered to "Smitty." The fat man on his belly and hanging on to Walker's left ankle, while squealing for Tom to help, went by the name of Ballard. These three spouted blood from lips, noses, and assorted gashes Walker inflicted on them.

Tom remained the only one calling him the spiteful names. The other three grew too engaged to spew their hate. So far, Walker managed to give 'em hell for all the names they'd used, but the fact remained his attackers moved him inch by inch closer to the rope dangling from a stout limb of a nearby oak tree.

"Why in the hell do we not just shoot him, Ballard?" Smitty asked through gritted teeth stained red with blood.

"We will hang him and then burn him," Ballard huffed, "Serves better to scare off any others of his kind that might trespass into these parts."

Tom still did not attempt going for Walker's kicking and stomping leg, but stopped the name calling just long enough to pick up a good-sized rock. Walker tried to turn in place as Tom circled, but just didn't have the remaining strength to turn his captors with him. As he expected, the rock soon collided with the back of his head.

The blow did not land sufficiently to knock him clean out. Still, it did hit hard enough to nearly buckle his knees. He all too quickly found himself beneath the rope and felt it tighten around his neck just before hearing roof beats of horses approaching at a trot.

"Hold up there, gentleman," a new voice called out.

"You two strangers need to keep on riding," Walker heard Ballard's voice respond through the haze filling his brain.

"Looks like you boys are about to hang a man who does not care to be hung," the unfamiliar voice responded.

"I fail to see that is any of your business, mister," Ballard barked.

"Probably not," the new voice responded, "but I've always been cursed with an overabundance of curiosity. What crime did this man commit?"

Smitty and the other man let go of Walker's arms and his mind started to clear from Tom's clobbering. Ballard kept a firm grip on the hoisting end of the rope around Walker's neck but didn't tug to cinch it so tight he couldn't turn in place to look up at the two men on horseback.

The self-proclaimed curious man rode a Paint mare and wore a large black hat with a crease in the middle of the crown. He didn't look to have much length to him, but was built broad of shoulder and thick through his chest and arms. The man beside him appeared to be simply an ordinary cowboy, but one mounted upon a large and magnificent buckskin.

"You ask what crime he committed?" Ballard snickered. "Why, hell mister, can you not tell by lookin'?"

"I did so dread that might be the case," the man on the Paint replied before casually pushing back his coattails to reveal the pearl handles of two Colts worn in cross- drawl fashion.

No common man sported pearl handles on his firearms, and the fact made the four men standing around Walker grow awfully serious real fast.

"That looks to be some fancy iron you be packin'," Ballard said uneasily.

"As a matter of fact, they are damned fancy," the man replied. "And damned special as well. These Colts once belonged to a man you might have heard tale of. His name was Clay Bardoe."

* * * *

"How the hell did you come to own Clay Bardoe's guns?" the man holding the hanging rope asked.

Floyd Danner unthreateningly pulled both Colts from the holsters and held them out for display with the barrels pointed to the blue skies overhead. Even though they were not looking down the barrels, the scoundrels of the lynching party noticeably tensed.

"Consider them presented to me as a gift by the gentleman who found it his regrettable duty to shoot and kill Clay Bardoe."

"CB Wooly gave you those guns?" the mob leader asked.

"He gave me this one," Danner replied with a wave of the Colt in his left hand, "I was one of his two deputies at the time. This one here," Danner emphasized with a wave of the other, "I picked up off the floor of a saloon where C.B. dropped it, just winks of an eye before a sorry cowardly kind of bastard shot him in the back. He then pissed on my dying friend. Not an act, I might mention, that won't be given serious consideration when I'm blessed to catch up with the afore mentioned sorry cowardly kind of bastard."

"I heard told that ol' CB went and got himself killed up there in No Man's Land," the leader said.

"That he did," Danner sighed.

"Is that what brings you into this part of the territory?" The leader asked.

"As a matter of fact, it is. I am looking for a man calling himself John Turner. I hear he is bartending yonder in Wewoka town."

"I don't get into town all that much, but I feel sure if he be there, you look capable enough of finding him. Ain't that many bars in Wewoka. Any how, I guess you two best get to your business and leave us to ours."

"Well, now, that is most likely what me and my pardner here ought to do," Danner chuckled, "but it just pains me to think a man might dangle from a rope simply because of the color of his skin."

"What are you? Some kind of darky lover?" The leader snarled.

Danner smiled at the man before lowering the Colts to point at his hateful face. "Don't know that I am, but I damned sure know I am a hater of mean and ugly white men." Danner kept the pistols on the man holding the rope but turned his eyes on the man at the other end. "Mister, are you willing to let this here mob hang you?"

The black man shook his head emphatically, "No, sir, I just as soon they lets me remain alive and kickin'."

Danner turned his eyes back to the leader. "Did you hear that? The man does not care to be strung-up today. Now, I ain't as good with these Colts as was Clay Bardoe or CB Wooly, but from this distance, I can take your face off. Please remove that noose from the gentleman's neck."

"Gentleman?" The leader hissed.

Danner pulled the hammer back on both pistols and the man mounted beside him jerked his Winchester from the scabbard and covered the other three. "They call my pardner here Hound. He is straddled a horse named Moonshine that first belonged to Bardoe and then Wooly. Hound does not say much, but he is damned handy with that rifle. You can get to releasing that man...or you can all get to dying."

The leader of the lynching mob got busy removing the noose from the black man's neck.

* * * *

Danner waited until they were safely out of gun range before turning to the man mounted on a bay mare. "I'm Floyd Danner and this is Hound Olivo. What would be your name?"

"My mamma and poppa named me Abe Lincoln Walker. I's born two months after General Lee surrendered at Appomattox Court House. I ain't never been no slave to no other man."

"Well, that is all good and fine and I'm glad to hear it," Danner responded, "But what do you prefer to be called... Abe...Lincoln...or Walker?"

"I'd prefer you call me Abe."

"Well, hello there, Abe."

"Hello, Mista Danner."

"No need in calling me anything but Floyd, Abe. Now, this quiet man here at my side, Hound Olivo, being the peculiar type, just might prefer you calling him Mr. Olivo. Would that be right, Hound?"

"Heck fire, Floyd, you know that ain't right. I never met a man insisting to be called mister that was not full of vainglory or shit. Abe, you can call me Hound. It ain't my true given name but might as well be."

Danner chuckled at Olivo's response. If left to his own, Hound Olivo might not utter a word in three days' time. Danner took to joshing him just to enjoy tidbits of the cowboy's dry wit.

Abe didn't appear to find any humor in the joshing or the response but seemed practically awe stricken. "Why glory be, I ain't never called a white man anything but mista."

"Now if you insist on calling me Mr. Danner, I'll be calling you Mr. Walker."

"Lordy! Lordy!" Abe howled, "A white man callin' a colored man mista? From what I just seen, that would get both the white man and the colored killed dead in these parts!"

"Well, you best call me Floyd then. And you best ride on into Wewoka with us in case those skunks think about giving chase."

Abe looked simply too deep in thought to even offer a response, but he kept his bay pointed in the direction of Wewoka. The three men traversed nearly a mile before Abe turned in his saddle to look at Danner.

"The man you be lookin' for in Wewoka, Mista Dan…uh…*Floyd*…is he the dangerous type?"

"He could be, Abe. The man has the skills to be mighty dangerous. Most men I've seen will go into a gunfight with their firearm at the ready, but he does not have to do that. He is quicker than a whore on payday. He is terribly accurate as well. I've seen him shoot holes clear through Lady Liberty on a dime tossed in the air."

"Hope you don't mind me saying so," Abe started with a definitive shake of his head, "but ten cents be a lot of money. Seem like a pitiful waste to me. But he do sound like a dangerous type. I's tell you right now, Floyd and Hound, ol' Abe Lincoln Walker here will stand right by you side in facing this rascal. I ain't never had no white man do me a good turn until you two stepped right up and saved my life. I ain't gonna be forgettin' that if I live to be as old as Moses."

"Oh, hell, Abe, I already got a feeling you are the make of man who would do the same for either of us," Danner smiled, impressed with his new acquaintance. "And I do appreciate your offer to help, but the matter between me and this man is personal. I intend to kill him all by myself, and it will be no great a challenge anyhow. He is damned skilled, but he has a yeller streak running down his back as wide as the ol' Mississippi."

"I done learned in my life, Floyd, the skeer'd types are apt to run in packs just like them mens back behind us. If you man do," Abe said while removing a long-gun from a saddle scabbard, "Ol' Abe will be tryin' out this here new scattergun 'cause Ol' Abe ain't skeer'd a no fight. I know when you first laid eyeballs on me them mens had me pretty near whipped down. But had you got there a few minutes earlier you would caught me givin' 'em hell."

Danner believed every word of it. Anytime one man fighting four could make three of them bleed as badly as Danner witnessed, that one man certainly had to be a formidable scrapper. After nodding his belief, Danner turned his eyes on the newfangled shotgun Abe held in display.

"That is one fine looking weapon. I have seen advertisements of the pump action Winchester, but never seen one put to use."

"This here be the Model 1897 twelve-gauge. I keeps it loaded with double-ought shells with smokeless powder. I can shoots five times fo having to reload and can throw a passel of shot in a skirmish and never be blinded by no smoke."

Danner watched as Abe slid the shotgun back into the scabbard, and then he pointed to the tall boots on the man's large feet. "Those are cavalry boots ain't they, Abe?"

"Yes, sir, sho is. I served my time with the Tenth Cavalry Regiment. Gots my discharge just last month and left Fort Leavenworth up in Kansas to come down here in the territory and buy me a piece of land to farm. I put back all mys pay and only used a little so far to buy this here horse and my shotgun."

"Sounds like a noble pursuit, Abe. There's no work more respectable than farming," Danner smiled as he turned his eyes on Hound but again addressed the new acquaintance. "And I find it damned refreshing to find a man that can carry on a conversation."

Hound never took his eyes off the road in front of them but said out the corner of his mouth, "I can carry on a conversation, Floyd. I just choose not to."

* * * *

The three horsemen reigned to a stop in front of a bricked structure on the main street of Wewoka. A large sign of considerable craftsmanship above the door identified the establishment as the Palladian Palace. Danner thought it certainly looked to be a place of class and distinction, but being only shortly after the dinner hour, it did not appear to be doing a brisk business. Word had it, that it would be in the Palladian Palace where Danner could find a mysteriously reserved bartender going by the name of John Turner.

"You boys care to join me for a swig?" Danner said as he swung from the saddle.

Hound dismounted willingly, but Abe remained in the saddle. Danner looked up at the ebony skinned man and grinned before saying, "Not a drinking man, Abe?"

"I's enjoyed a gulp or two of moonshine from time to time, Floyd, but don't recon I's be welcomed in such a fancy sort of place."

Danner turned and studied the outer façade of the proclaimed palace before turning back to the still mounted man. "Abe, I see no signs restricting a dark-skinned man."

"Do not mean theys don't restrict us all the same," Abe responded.

"Well, it comes down to this, Abe. Do you desire to go in there with Hound and me to enjoy a drink or two…maybe three, depending on who we may or may not find?"

"Truth be, Floyd, I desires to go and do and be treated like any other man."

"Then crawl your ass down and bring it along," Danner chuckled. "Any sort behind those walls having trouble with you will have trouble with me and Hound as well. Ain't that right, Hound?"

"Yup," Hound grumbled.

"Abe," Danner grinned, "That is Hound Olivo's way of inviting you kindly to crawl your ass down and bring it along."

Abe winced and emitted a groan, but did in fact dismount.

Danner tethered his Paint and then pulled the pearl-handled Colt from his left holster with his right hand and concealed it behind the lapel of his coat and beneath his left arm pit. "I'll go in first. If the scoundrel is behind the bar, I intend to shoot him, and then we can have our drinks."

Only a handful of patrons filled the dusky interior. The man behind the bar was not the man Danner sought, but he approached him all the same to inquire about another bartender hiding behind a name that he did not own. He didn't make it up to the finely polished mahogany bar before the attending barkeep pointed a finger back behind Danner and announced with authority, "We do not allow niggers in the Palladian."

Danner stopped a few paces in front of the bar and cocked his head to employee his most menacing look before dropping to his side the hand holding the Colt. The bartender quickly averted his eyes from Abe to the gun in Danner's hand.

"Do you own this place?" Danner asked calmly.

"Uh…no."

"Then I am guessing you ain't willing to bleed for another man's rules. Could that be true?"

The man behind the bar exhibited no outwardly characteristics of either bravery nor stupidity. "If I serve him, mister, I will surely lose my job."

Danner placed the Colt back in its holster. "We'll take a table in the back. You bring me your finest bottle of rye whiskey and I will serve him my own damned self."

The bartender wasted no time in getting the bottle to the table. Danner handed the man twice what the whiskey cost and told him to keep the remainder. While the man nervously placed three glasses on the table, Danner stared into twitching eyes and said, "I hear another bartender by the name of Turner works here. Where can I find him?"

This bartender seemed to be combating a need to swallow his tongue, and his words came haltingly. "John will be relieving me in about an hour and a half. Or should be, if'n he ain't drunk again. He stays drunk most of the time." The man then looked up at Danner's hat and scanned his eyes over Danner's upper torso. "By that big black hat and your stout build, I assume your name is Floyd Danner. John's been expecting you. Told me to send someone to warn him if'n you ever showed up."

"But you won't be doing that," Danner grinned, "Will you?"

The bartender swallowed hard a few times and finally cleared his throat before responding, "No, sir. I do not choose to do that."

"Leave us to our bottle then," Danner mumbled.

The man made it back behind his bar and busied himself swabbing out glasses before Abe looked Danner hard in the eyes. "I's ain't never known a white man like you."

Danner didn't have a response. Surprisingly, Hound did. "That could be a good thing, Abe."

The three men threw back their first drink from the bottle before Abe spoke again. "Ain't none of mines business, but I would sho-nough like to know why it is you huntin' this man Turner."

"Abe, back under that tree where those bastards intended to hang you, the names of Clay Bardoe and CB Wooly were mentioned. Did the names mean anything to you?"

"No, Sir, ain't never heard of neither."

"A long time ago, they were both U.S. Deputy Marshals and loyal pardners. Clay Bardoe was an acclaimed shootist, but he always shot to wound. He had a problem with killing when killing wasn't necessary. One day, a man he should have killed when he had a chance, but let him live instead, snuck up on him and shot him three times in the back. Clay would have died had a woman named Millie not nursed him back to life. He ended up marrying this woman, gave up his badge and gun, and took up store keeping.

"Life at that point and time was damned good for ol' Clay. He loved his Millie something awfully. Then one day a bunch of evil men killed Millie in a terrible fashion, but not before defiling her in a disgusting manner. Something busted wide open in Clay and he went into a killing frenzy. Didn't stop until each of those men paid for their sins with their lives. As a result, Clay found himself on the wrong side of the law, and it fell to CB Wooly and his pardner at the time, Walt Tabor, to bring Clay to justice. It turned out that this Tabor...*was not up to the task...*" Danner paused and tried to extinguish a fire in his guts with another shot of whiskey. "Turned out, CB Wooly had to take on his old friend Clay Bardoe all by himself. In a truly miraculous sort of way, CB bested Clay and shot him dead in a saloon in Stillwater. CB became notorious for that fight. Hell, books were written about him. Because of his fame, he was invited to clean up Beaver City up in No Man's Land. He hired me, and his old partner, Walt Tabor, to serve as his deputies."

Danner paused to throw down yet another shot of whiskey. "I had a real problem with CB bringing on Tabor, because, in short, he run out on him once and I expected he could do the same again. But CB was damned intent on giving the man another chance. Up there in Beaver City, we got cross with some hired killers and a rancher named Stew Graybow, who is a sorry son of a bitch of the highest order. Sure enough, Walt Tabor ran out on us. Because of circumstances I could not control, CB ended up shooting it out with the hired killers all by himself. He did not kill them, but they didn't kill him either. He was shot all to hell, but did not die until Graybow stuck a gun in his back and shot him another three times.

"Now, Abe, I am out to track down and bring to justice those hired guns and the bastard Stew Graybow. Before doing that, I intend to fulfill a promise I made to Walt Tabor. That being, if he were to run out on CB yet again, which he did, I would find him and shoot him dead. Hound and I have hunted high and low for Tabor for over a year, and learned recently, that he now calls himself John Turner. I intend to fulfill my promise to him in less than an hour and a half."

Danner watched as Abe glanced down and stared into the amber-colored liquid in the glass resting between his powerful looking hands. "Lordy, Lordy," Abe clucked.

"Yup," Danner agreed.

Abe took a sip from his glass and then turned his eyes on Hound. "Ifs you don't mind me askin', Hound, how you fits in all this?"

"I worked as a ranch hand for Stew Graybow. I am good at tracking. Kind of like a hound. Floyd asked me to help him find the men he needs to kill. I figure they need to be killed."

"Lordy, Lordy," Abe hummed yet again.

"Yup," Hound nodded.

Danner shook his head and chuckled at the quiet man he'd come to deeply admire. "Hound, Tabor could be coming anytime. He will for sure notice my Paint and Moonshine. Could I trouble you to move them out of sight? I could do it myself, but I want to be here and shoot him the minute he walks through that door."

"I's move them horses," Abe volunteered.

Hound beat him to his feet. "I need to stretch my legs anyway," he said before heading toward the door.

* * * *

Danner sat alongside Abe and both men paid more attention to the liquor than they did each other. "I's ain't never had white man's fine whiskey befoe," Abe said after enough time had come and gone for Hound to return from his task. "It some damned good stuff. I's be willin' to pay you for the amount I's guzzled."

"Should our paths ever cross again, Abe Lincoln Walker, you can buy the next bottle," Danner winked.

Abe worked himself into a beaming smile at about the same moment an assortment of angry voices and the pounding of numerous stomping boot heels prompted both men to turn their attention to the saloon door. Danner had his hands on the table preparing to hoist himself to his feet when Hound Olivo came partially flying, but mostly stumbling, through the entrance in a state of near unconsciousness. His floppy and sweat stained hat sat his head at a disheveled angle and blood nearly covered his face. Danner had not yet coordinated what his eyes saw with what his brain deducted before a troop of men pushed through the opening behind Hound. He had only time to wrap his hands around his holstered firearms before realizing an assortment of pistols, rifles, and shotguns beat him to the drawl.

At the head of the mob of eight stood the man named Ballard holding a Colt Navy aimed somewhere between Danner's eyes and nose. "Pull those guns belonging to Clay Bardoe," he hissed, "and me and all my kin will send you to hell you nigra lovin' sonabitch!"

Die here inside or die somewhere outside. It clearly came down to that, but Danner under the influence of too much fine white man's liquor took too long in making the decision. A lasso flew forward to land around his neck. In the mere seconds that followed he found himself jerked off his feet and pulled across the table to land sprawled on the hardwood floor, where members of the gang of eight treated him to blows to the head from the butts of their guns. Dazed to near blacking out, he could not stop them from stripping away his prized Colts. Danner retained just enough of his senses to realize poor Abe, too, had been lassoed, taken down, and beat about the head in the same fashion as Danner.

* * * *

Such would not have happened to CB Wooly. He would've been prepared and quicker to take action, and Danner felt foolish as well as inadequate for his poor showing. With hands trussed behind their backs, Danner, his pardner Hound, and their new acquaintance Abe Walker were jerked from the saloon and tugged down the street by the nooses around their necks. All too quickly they ended up beneath a towering oak tree beside a livery stable on the outskirts of Wewoka. Convinced he'd soon be dangling from a branch of the tree, Danner prepared to offer his apologies to Hound and Abe for failing them so miserably. Before he could put together his words, a familiar voice called out from beyond the tangle of men going about the tasks of their lynching.

"Drop them ropes and your guns and get your hands in the air!"

Danner craned his neck in the direction from where the order had been issued to find a man in bartending garb standing with his feet spread shoulder length apart and his hands down along the sides of his legs. The thumbs of both hands rested on the hammers of Colt Peacemakers pointed only at the ground beneath his feet.

"Why hell," the gang leader Ballard responded, "You ain't nothin' but a bartender, and a drunk to boot!"

"Before I was a bartender," the man called back, "I was the cowardly son of a bitch known by the name of Walt Tabor. That is why I presently go by the name of Turner. Not because I'm hiding from what I got coming to me, but because I long ago grew tired of being known as the coward I truly by nature be. But I don't presently feel cowardly. Do as I say, or I'll surely kill you where you stand."

An entire assortment of mixed emotions washed over Danner. He did not care to die by hanging, nor did he particularly cherish the thought of being saved by a man he'd dedicated himself to killing. He had yet to sort through his dilemma when his captors drew a collective conclusion that one cowardly drunk of a bartender could not match an assortment of eight firearms.

Danner along with Hound and Abe could do no more than dance in place as all hell broke loose. Ballard and his men let go with pistols, rifles and shotguns only to end up either falling to the dirt or turning to run as Walt Tabor stood his ground and precisely placed his shots while returning fire.

The gunfight ended as quickly as it began. Two men, including Ballard, lay strewn still and dead at Danner's feet while three more thrashed and moaned on the ground beneath the big Oak. The other three managed to flee the killing field, and Danner figured regrouping to be the furthest thing from their minds. If eight men could not take down one opponent, what could three possibly hope to do, but end up like the other five?

Abe Hunter muttered the first words after the smoke cleared, and Danner could not have summed the results more precisely.

"Lordy, Lordy, good God almighty!"

CHAPTER TWO

Bygones be Bygones

Tabor tucked the Colts into the waist band of his trousers and forced himself to turn his eyes on Floyd Danner and meet his stare. Tabor recognized the cowboy from Graybow's Four Deuces ranch up in No Man's Land, but could not recall his name. He'd never seen the black man before. The three stood side by side beneath the Oak with their hands bound behind their backs. The cowhand and the stranger were paying more attention to the carnage than they were Tabor, but not so with Danner. The short and stout man locked his eyes on Tabor, but didn't offer any words to clarify the meaning of a glare not totally comprised of hatred.

Tabor saw no need of expressing his thoughts either, but silently walked up and stepped behind Floyd to loosen his hands. Floyd turned to face Tabor while rubbing at the friction marks on his wrists. Tabor pulled the Colts from his trousers, twirled them in his hands, and extended them butts up for Floyd's taking.

"I have grown weary of living with my conscience. Take these and do what you came here to do. No man would have ever done me a greater favor."

Floyd stared long and hard at the offered Colts before turning without a word and untying the hands of his two companions. He then stepped up to Ballard's corpse and used the toe of his boot to flip the man from his stomach onto his back. Floyd reached down and removed two pearl handled Colts tucked beneath the dead man's gun belt. Tabor immediately recognized the guns once belonging to Clay Bardoe. The very guns which a couple of years before cast upon Tabor an infamous constitution and reputation he seemed cursed to carry to his grave.

"You save my life," Floyd grumbled as he straightened, "and that of these two fine men…and then you have the gall to burden me with freeing you from your miserable existence. If I live to be a very old man, Walt Tabor, I will never understand your way of thinking…or behaving."

"You came here to kill me, Floyd. What happened here today does not change your right to do that. I am only half sober now, but in my right mind. Do me the respect of putting me out of my misery."

"And what kind of sorry son of a bitch would that now make me?" Floyd hissed before turning to the cowboy and expressing frustration. "Hound, could you please explain to me how a man can turn tail and run from two men one day and then take a stand to fight eight on yet another?"

The cowboy, Tabor now remembered as Hound Olivo, shuffled about uncomfortably before responding, "Since you push me for an answer, Floyd, I must admit it confuses my mind. But I'm more thankful that he did, than concerned as to how or why he did."

"My point exactly, Hound," Floyd said with an exasperated shake of his head. "Now, how can I go and kill a man after doing such?"

"Don't rightly think you can, Floyd," Hound sighed.

"Abe," Floyd said to the other man, "What is your thinking on the situation?"

"Floyd, I's just be thinkin' it a miracle from God above that I's been saved from two hangin's in one day by white fellers. I's fear killin' this man now would be a terrible pity... Lordy, Lordy... just a terrible pity and maybe a sin to boot."

Floyd wheeled to look Tabor hard in the eyes once again. "That about sums it, Walt. Killing you today ain't no longer an option. So, where the hell does that leave us?"

Tabor took a deep breath and fought to remain upright on his feet. For over a year now, he'd lived only for this moment. He'd existed only to die. An hour had passed since his last drink. His mind had yet to clear from the fog and only one option seemed acceptable. He lifted one of the Colts and thrust it to the side of his head.

"If you can not or will not do it, then I will surely do it myself. I won't walk a step from where I now stand."

The men around him were not the gasping types, but all did clearly take pause. Danner seemed reluctant, but took one step closer. His response proved typically brash.

"I can think of no better way to stamp Walt Tabor eternally a coward. Pull that trigger and prove forever the accusations that have scorned your name."

"What better thing can I do?"

Danner momentarily offered a response seemingly as bitter to utter as the taste of vinegar. "The men responsible for the death of CB Wooly still breathe air they don't deserve to cherish. You can go with us and revenge his death. If you're not willing to do your just part, then pull that damned trigger."

"Should I go, where would that leave you and me?"

"Just know here and now that I once got to a point where I considered you a friend…I will never get to that point again."

"Should we find these men, do you intend to deal with them justly, or simply kill them where they stand?"

"Why should that matter to you?" Danner growled.

"I haven't abandoned all that I have stood for in the past. I can be called fittingly many names, but I've yet to be called a murderer."

Danner sighed hard and took on the appearance of a man wrestling the devil. "If they choose to face a jury, I will grant them that undeserved right."

"That being the case…I will ride with you."

Floyd stood clearly conflicted. Half sober or not, Tabor could read it in his eyes.

"Laughing Billy Bemo and that killing Apache will be no less dangerous or capable than they were in Beaver City, and Stew Graybow will likely surround himself with hired guns. How do I know you won't run out again?"

"You don't know…and neither do I. I reckon that to be a river we'll have to ford when and if we come to it."

"Hound," Floyd barked, "Do we want him riding with us?"

It seemed to Tabor that Hound felt pained to yet again be dragged into discussion. "I never recall seeing no man shoot the way he can shoot. If he can stand at our side, we'd surely have a leg up on those killers. If he won't or can't….well, we couldn't be no worse off than we are right now with just the two of us."

Tabor waited for Floyd's response, but the man called Abe spoke first.

"That would be the three of us, Hound."

"What are you saying, Abe?" Floyd asked.

"I's reckon to be sayin' I's want to throw in with you mens, if you'd be havin' me."

"What about your farming, Abe?" Floyd asked.

"Ol' Mother Earth's been here a long time, Floyd. I's be bettin' she'll still be 'round after this work is done and I's be bettin' I's still can buy a spot of her for farmin' even then."

"Abe, I would be honored to have you along with us. But you need to know these men we hunt are of the worst types. There will be a lot of blood shed, and I fear they might not be the only ones doing the bleeding."

"I's done some bleedin' befoe, Floyd. Besides, I's owe you and Hound here and even this other man my life. Way's I's see it, I's got some payin' back to do."

Floyd grinned while shaking Abe's hand, but the grin faded away when he turned to Tabor. "I learned here today not to make threats I might not be able to carry out. I just ask you kindly, Walt Tabor, do not run out on me again."

Tabor truly desired to offer a response, but he too knew how easily a man might say and think one thing, only to later find himself helpless to do yet another. Instead he asked a question.

"Where do we go from here, Floyd?"

Danner pointed to the west. "We hope to add one more to our number. We are riding to find Zed Martin, formally of the Tackett Ranch. He found the bastard Bemo and brought him to Beaver City. I can only assume he can find him again."

Tabor looked from Danner to Olivo. "Do you not consider Martin an enemy, Hound?"

Olivo shrugged and replied, "I'm willing to let bygones be bygones."

Tabor could not help but wonder if they'd find the cowboy Martin harboring the same sentiments.

* * * *

It didn't take long for Tabor to gather what he'd need, and the four now sat their saddles ready to pull out. Danner took note that Tabor altered his dress by only adding a low crowned derby.

"The last I laid eyes on you, Walt, you wore the finery of a dime-novel shootist. Do you no longer own such dandy clothing?"

Tabor ducked his head and sighed before offering his response. "Even if I did, I wouldn't wear them. I no longer harbor grand illusions of what I am, but know clearly what I am not."

The meaning of Tabor's self-debasement offered in bare-boned honesty, poked Danner like the pointed end of a sharp knife, bringing him to remember his own stark realization of not an hour in the passing. He turned his eyes from Tabor to scan the faces of the other two men who certainly looked to him for leadership.

"Before we ride from here, I best say what needs to be said," Danner started by staring down at his saddle horn, "That being, that I sat in that saloon, and was too easily taken because I have not the quality of a C.B. Wooly or a Clay Bardoe. What happened to me, wouldn't have happened to either of them. As a result, good men who have voluntarily put themselves in my charge nearly died."

Danner looked up to find the other three men displaying quizzical expressions seemingly demanding that he say more. The truth being, no other words seemed necessary.

"What is your point, Floyd?" Tabor finally asked.

"Why, hell-fire, Walt, my point is that I am not C.B. Wooly or Clay Bardoe."

"You done tole me," Abe chimed in, "That them fellas is long dead, Floyd."

"Of course, they are dead, Abe. If they were alive we would not be having this discussion because none of this would be necessary."

"Well, then," Abe grinned brightly, "I's glad you ain't them. Dead men don't do nobody not good, cep'n the worms."

Danner exhaled a breath of utter frustration before asking, "Are you boys ready to ride?"

"We could have been five minutes down the trail already," Hound deadpanned, "If'n it hadn't been for all this talking."

Danner clucked to his horse and turned the Paint to the west before looking to the sky above and declaring, "Lord help us."

* * * *

Laughing Billy Bemo ducked into the rear door of the apothecary's office.

The proprietor, with his back to this door, stood behind his counter mixing some concoction. Startled, he whipped around and noticeably tensed even more at the sight of the buckskin clad Bemo.

"Is it done?" the apothecary Dayne Williams all but gasped.

Bemo just being Bemo threw back his head and cackled. "Hellfire, Williams, would I be here if it were not so?"

The small and thin business man closed his eyes and took a deep trembling breath as he began ringing his hands.

"Too late for all that nonsense," Bemo giggled. "Just get to gettin' my money so I can skedaddle."

Williams opened his eyes and directed them at the three Remington revolvers visible for his viewing. Two rested butts forward in holsters. The third Bemo wore tucked into the front of his gun belt.

Williams knew Bemo carried a fourth one secured in the same belt but in the small of his back.

"Did she suffer?" Williams' voice quaked.

"You said you wanted her to. So, she did," Bemo tittered.

Williams nodded his head nervously, but seemingly satisfied, before crossing the room and bending to open his safe, intentionally blocking Bemo's view of the combination he employed. Once Williams leaned forward to reach into the open safe, Bemo moved quickly toward him, grabbed the collar of his suit coat and jerked him over backwards to tumble onto the planked floor.

Williams managed only to squeal a frantic objection before Bemo turned to the door he'd entered and bellowed, "Get on in here now!"

The fine-looking woman with dark hair tied into a bun burst through the door and slammed it shut behind her.

"Deborah!" Williams gasped from his place on the floor.

Bemo slapped his right thigh in laughter while pulling one of the Remingtons with the other hand. He leaned to thrust the barrel beneath William's chin before commanding, "Get the money, woman. Every last dollar of it!"

"But I don't understand," Williams babbled.

"It ain't all that perplexing," Bemo giggled. "You offered me only three hundred to kill your wife here, but she told me you had five or six times that in your safe. Besides, she is much too pretty to put bullets in!"

Williams began sobbing and his words came in tearful bursts. "She was unfaithful…took another man…now she has betrayed me yet again!"

"I like a woman who spreads it around," Bemo laughed. "I reckon if she will give it out to one man, she will give it up for me as well. I got the widow woman waiting at home for me, but don't expect she might object too much to me bringing back a stray. She can't argue that ol' Laughing Billy's man enough to satisfy two gals."

"Deborah! You are going with him?" Williams babbled.

"Better than letting him kill me," the woman mumbled without looking up from her task of emptying the safe.

"But…but…what about me?" Williams sobbed.

"Why, hell, Williams," Bemo guffawed, "You will be dead."

The cuckolded apothecary had only enough time to gasp in dread before Bemo thumbed back the hammer and pulled the trigger.

* * * *

"So, you are the man who wrote them books about CB Wooly killing Clay Bardoe?"

David Hathcoat looked down at the much older man with stark white hair and a long beard sitting at the table in front of him. Nervously, his eyes darted to the five rough looking characters standing aligned behind the stern old man. Hathcoat doubted that an entire squad of federal troops carried more firearms than what adorned the five ruffians.

"I did indeed pen the exploits of Marshal CB Wooly," the portly Hathcoat responded, taking care to subdue the arrogance of his noted stature as a writer of great acclaim.

"Do you know who I am?" the white-haired man snarled.

"I can only assume you are the gentleman that summoned me to this remote location," Hathcoat answered, forcing himself not to refer to the shabby saloon in southern Kansas as an enclave in the bowels of hell. Hathcoat traveled here only after being promised by telegraph to meet the sole eye witness of the tragic death befalling the subject of his most prosperous series of books.

The westerner before him practically smiled before announcing haughtily, "I am the man who killed CB Wooly. My name is Stew Graybow, but you'll address me as Mr. Graybow."

Even if the old man hadn't a team of killer types at his back, Hathcoat would not have objected to the edict. Hathcoat hailed from Boston, but spent enough time in these ruthless regions to know better than to equate old age with frailty. Despite his advanced years, Graybow exhibited a continence of a man best not angered.

Hathcoat carefully chose his response and delivered it humbly, intentionally not relaying all he'd heard about the shoot out in Beaver City. "I was led to believe Marshal Wooly died at the hands of an Indian and a crazed killer known for his jolly demeanor."

"Bumbling jackasses the both of them!" Graybow huffed. "Wooly shot them to hell, and it fell to me to kill the meddling bastard my own self. I summoned you here thinking you might want to write the story of a famed Indian fighter and rancher who faced down and killed the sorry son of a bitch you previously and wrongly portrayed as a hero."

Regardless of the truth, the old rancher's version would sell like picks and shovels during a gold rush. Besides, Hathcoat's readers proved to prefer grandeur fiction over the often less spectacular and boring truth.

"I can certainly transpose your story to riches, Mr. Graybow," Hathcoat said before bowing to display servitude.

"I don't object to money, Hathcoat," Graybow grumbled, "but what I most desire is having my story told."

"And told it shall be, Mr. Graybow," Hathcoat replied with a forced smile.

* * * *

Laughing Billy Bemo reigned his horse to a stop in front of the decaying little cabin he'd come to call home. The horse he straddled, once belonging to a Texas ranger he'd killed, stood directly over the grave of the farmer who'd built the cabin. Bemo, too, had killed the farmer in order to make the farmer's wife his own.

"Hey Widow Woman!" Bemo called out in laughter toward the cabin while remaining in the saddle.

The door to the cabin opened and a disheveled blonde-headed woman in tattered clothing stepped out into the waning light of day. She looked first to Bemo with a look of indifference before turning her head to stare at the dark-haired woman on the horse beside him.

"Widow Woman," Bemo giggled, "This here is Debbie. She is gonna be living here with us from now on and will be sharing in your responsibility of making me a happy man!"

The mounted woman at Bemo's side glared down at the blonde and announced, "My name is Deborah."

The woman in the front of the door responded insolently, "My name is Marge, but he has always called me nothing but Widow Woman. You best know your name is now Debbie."

Bemo threw back his head and laughed heartily. Neither woman joined him in his glee, but little did that matter. He drew his right leg over the saddle and leapt to the ground before commanding, "You gals see to the horses. They had a hard day of riding, and use your efforts to get to know each other. Then I will be needing supper and some wifely attention. Do not particularly care if provided by one or both!"

CHAPTER THREE

Becoming the Hunter

Two days had come and nearly gone since he'd performed his act of mercy on the ancient Kiowa woman. Soon the sun would complete its day's work only to surrender mother earth to the moon and allowing the Apache to reach his destination in the hours of darkness. The deepness of night suited the Apache. He performed best his occupation while cloaked in darkness, stepping from shadows to catch his victim unaware.

Thoughts of his intended deed occupied the hired killer's mind, rendering him unprepared for the man who sprung from the brush at the side of the road with a Winchester rifle at the ready.

"Drop either hand from your reins, and I'll a bullet through your chest," the man announced.

The man in the road could not know the mistake he'd made. He clearly did not understand it best for most men, not including the Apache, to first shoot, and only then talk if talking still proved necessary. In that the man with the rifle already proved himself inferior, the Apache known by many names calmly halted his coal black stallion and sat easy in his saddle.

"I assume you to be a highway man," the Apache scoffed, "and not one of great wisdom. I will prove to be no easy man to rob."

"I am no thief, you murdering bastard! My name is Jack Jones…the man you intend to kill."

Only now did the Apache grow tense. The Jones homestead stood a good ten miles up the road he traveled. Never before had an intended victim shown the initiative to interrupt the killer's planned attack. He didn't know until now the feeling of helplessness that accompanied the moment the prey seized the opportunity to become the aggressor. The Apache took a long moment to consider his predicament before drawing a truly inspired conclusion.

Slowly and oh so carefully, the Apache turned his stallion in the road, giving his back to Jack Jones and starting his horse at a walk in the direction from wince he'd traveled.

"What the hell are you doing?" Jones shouted.

The Apache turned his head over his shoulder to holler back his response. "I have learned a lesson this day. I am sparing your life."

The Apache, like Jack Jones, knew of men intending to hunt him down and send him into what awaits the dead. Until now, he'd somehow grown foolishly complacent, and practically content to let those men go about the task of finding him. Jack Jones served to awaken the Apache to the realization that the hunted stood much greater chances of survival by becoming the hunter.

"How do you know I don't intend shoot you in the back?" Jones called out.

The bullets of another white man in the not too distant past served to make the Apache think he'd lost his medicine. But instead of lost, it suddenly proved only to have temporarily taken leave, only to return now fully rejuvenated.

"Mr. Jones, you have looked into the eyes of the angel of death," the Apache responded confidently. "Look into them again and you will not leave this place to talk about it."

Jack Jones clearly took the warning to heart, and the Apache left him to remain among the living.

* * * *

The sun had long set and a hearty supper of stew and cornbread served to prepare Zed Martin for a good night's rest. He'd just stretched out on his cot in the bunkhouse when a fellow hand called his name.

"Zed, there's a gaggle of riders outside saying they wish to speak to you. They look to be a serious lot. Ain't sure they might not be a posse. Guess you best crawl from that bunk and respond to their summons."

Martin felt more curious than worried. Best he could recall, he'd done nothing recently to require fearing a posse. He moved out the door and onto the long porch to indeed find a mounted gaggle. The moon and stars didn't provide enough light for Martin to identify any of the four riders.

"If you be looking for Zed Martin, you found him. I ain't wronged nobody, so what do you men want with me?"

"Zed, you know all but one of us four," the rider on the far right called out. "I am Floyd Danner, and I got with me Hound Olivo, Walt Tabor, and a new friend who prefers to be called Abe."

Curiosity settled and worry took its place for Martin. "Deputy Danner, I took no part in any of those killins' back in Beaver City, and though I don't feel especially friendly toward Hound, he can vouch for that if only he will."

"I vouch for that as the truth," another voice called out from the four. "And I hold no grudge against you, Zed Martin."

"I appreciate your honesty, Hound, but it was you who brought that terrible Apache to kill good friends of mine."

"And it was you, Zed, who fetched that crazy laughing bastard to kill my friends," Hound responded. "But like me, you just followed your orders."

Martin dropped his head and shook it sadly. "You make a solid point, Hound, and if I had it all to do over, I would not have followed those orders."

"Then that puts us square," Hound responded softly. "I regret the day I brought that murderous Indian to No Man's Land."

"That pretty much sums it all up, boys," Floyd's voice inserted. "That mess cost us all considerably, and that's why we are here now, Zed. We intend to bring the responsible scoundrels to pay for our losses. We want you to lead us to Laughing Billy Bemo. I hope to either see him hang or shoot him dead right along with the Apache and Stew Graybow."

Martin took a moment to consider his involvement. Several questions came to mind, and he asked the most pressing. "Hound? You plan to help him find Stew Graybow?"

"I do."

Martin took long and silent moments to make up his mind. "Well, if you are willing to do your part, that would make me a sorry kind a' so and so not to do mine. But, I must tell you all now, I am willing to take you where I last found Laughing Billy, but I can't take a hand in killing him."

"And why would that be, Zed?" Danner asked, expressing surprise.

"The one and only time I laid eyes upon that damned Apache, Laughing Billy told him I was his brother. Had he not done that, I'd be as dead as the rest of my pards this very minute."

"That is an honorable enough reason if there ever was one," Danner said. "You lead us to him, and we'll do our damndest to do the killing piece."

Martin nodded his head before saying, "You all are welcome to spend the night here. In the morning I can settle things with my boss, and then ride with you fellers to right my wrongs."

* * * *

"You agree it's right to go after Bemo first?"

"You're asking me?"

"Just you and me here right this moment," Danner huffed, "Who else would I be asking?"

"You haven't said ten words to me since leaving Wewoka two days past," Walt Tabor said before taking a sip of coffee from his tin cup. "The fact you now ask my opinion leaves me just a little confused."

Danner took a sip from his cup as well. Until this very moment, he'd not cared to converse with Walt. He still considered the man a despicable coward, but he could not deny that Walt held more experience in man hunting than did himself. Besides, the former U.S. Deputy Marshall, cowardly or not, proved in the past to be a deep kind of thinker with more than his fair share of smarts.

Danner swallowed a little pride along with the strong black coffee. "It seems since I put this little party together that I'm in charge of it. And I've already expressed my misgivings on leadership. All things considered, you are the most qualified to be my second in charge. If you don't want the responsibility, or don't want me asking your opinion, all you got to do is say so. Besides, you've been sober this entire time. That alone speaks of your willingness to change."

Walt stared into the black liquid in his cup long seconds before offering his response. "I've remained sober because I have nothing stronger to drink than this swill. That being what it is, and considering Zed's words last night, I feel as if I have more wrongs to right than any man here. I don't care to be in charge of anything or anybody, but I intend to help any way I can. If it's my opinion you want, I'll give it."

"Then get to it."

Walt nodded and took a deep breath before saying, "We have no clear idea where Graybow is. We believe the Apache is in New Mexico Territory, and Bemo is down in Texas. We stand closer to Texas than New Mexico."

"So, you agree on Bemo being first?"

"That is my opinion."

Danner fought off a cantankerous urge to announce they'd instead mount up for New Mexico. "I will get the others rounded up. We'll then head south and east to Texas."

* * * *

David Hathcoat trailed in his buggy behind the horses of Stew Graybow and his five henchmen as they entered the fairly civilized town of Wichita, Kansas. The frontier community couldn't compare to the eastern cities more to the noted author's likings, but it certainly had to be better than the mud-caked settlement they'd abandoned on the border of Kansas and the Oklahoma Territory.

Hathcoat hoped he would by now have warmed to the man whose story he'd agreed to write, but Graybow so far exhibited no characteristics Hathcoat cared to embrace. Such had not been the case with the lawman CB Wooly. From the very start of their contractual arrangement, Hathcoat sensed Wooly to be a man of character. Never once did it pain his conscience to immortalize the man in written word. Hathcoat might have sensationalized the historical account, but not once did he find himself needing to exaggerate on Wooly's motives or abilities.

The greatest difference he'd so far noted between Graybow and Wooly centered on the fact the former wantonly performed his defining kill. Not so with the latter. Hathcoat made Wooly famous for killing an infamous gunman and killer named Clay Bardoe. The writer believed with all his heart, that CB Wooly did so only because he could do nothing else. Wooly proved to be a hero in the true sense of the word, a fact that needed no embellishment by Hathcoat.

Such would not be the case with Graybow. The author and subject had yet to discuss exactly how Graybow closed the final chapter of CB Wooly's life, but Hathcoat took from other accounts that the deed certainly bore no heroics and bordered on despicable. How Graybow would want it recorded, Hathcoat could not imagine, and dreaded the day the topic demanded attention.

For the time being, Hathcoat intended no more than to enjoy the respite from the horrid to enjoy luxuries of a more sophisticated setting, albeit Wichita, and albeit in an establishment which Hathcoat's stories about CB Wooly brought notoriety. Hathcoat considered Graybow's desire to spend time at the Peacock Saloon and Hotel ironic in the least. That Graybow hoped to spend said time in the company of the harlot Martha Henry, Hathcoat deemed mostly fanatical. The Madame Henry's preference for younger men long stood as a fact known far and wide. Hathcoat's curiosity to witness Graybow's most likely ill-fated hopes, nearly matched the dread he held for meeting Martha Henry. His portrayal of her in CB Wooly's chronicles, although mostly accurate, had been less than flattering.

In his stories, he'd recorded the relationship between Henry and Dallas Babb, a thief and murderer with illusions of grandeur. Martha watched her young Babb die at the hands of his uncle, Clay Bardoe, in Oklahoma Territory. She'd also been present on the day CB Wooly found no other course than to end Clay Bardoe's life. Hathcoat could not have told the tales of Wooly without tying them to the selfish endeavors of the Wichita madam. What role the woman proved to play in the telling of Stew Graybow's life, was yet to be revealed. Hathcoat, however, intended to stand at the ready with pen and paper in hand.

* * * *

"I'll be damned if I'll put up with such a ruckus much longer," Bemo did his best to chuckle.

The widow woman and Debbie were going at it yet again. Bemo first considered it entertainment, if not a necessity for the women to determine their pecking order. But for the third time, punches, kicks, and hair pulling disturbed his peace. The widow woman prevailed in the first two bouts, but it seemed Debbie gained on earning the upper hand this time. Bemo let it go until he could no longer stand the piercing screams and profanity. He pulled a gun and put a bullet through the roof. The women released their grips from one another and turned ugly scowls Bemo's way.

"That is just what we need," widow woman screeched, "Another damn hole in the roof!"

"I cannot tolerate this another moment," Debbie wailed, "The stench, the squalor, the humiliation!"

Out of sheer frustration, Bemo released a howl of laughter before shooting yet another hole in the roof and pulling another revolver to fill his free hand. He pointed one of the pistols at the widow woman and the other at Debbie. Staring down barrels hushed both women's mouths.

"Gals, I want to tell you a story of yet another woman I once shared a bed with," Bemo snickered. "A Mexican woman named, Camilla. She carried in her belly my baby, but still decided to turn me into the Texas Rangers. I cared for her as much as I do either of you. Yet, I slit her throat, and watched her bleed out."

The various expressions of horror on the women's faces induced heart-felt laughter from Bemo. The moment it died away, he turned uncharacteristically somber.

"Choose to be happy, ladies, or… choose to follow the path of Camilla."

* * * *

In the glory days, or inglorious days depending on one's perspective of the Chisholm Trail, large groups of men entering the Peacock drew not a single eye of interest. Those days now long in the past, patrons mostly entered singularly or in pairs. When six rough looking men entered followed by a seventh, dressed in refined fashion, they did in fact draw the attention of Madam Martha Henry. Not all business proved good business, and the madam approached the men with a leery eye. With the exception of the dandy, the group seemed a gang with the obvious leader being the much older man with a long and snow-white beard.

"Good afternoon *gentlemen*, and welcome to the Peacock," Martha said with an air of intended suspicion. "I am the Madam Martha Henry. How may I be of your service?"

The older man with penetrating cold blue eyes gave Martha a once-over, providing an obvious appreciation she seldom these days earned. The eyes exhibited an alertness of a much younger man, and the older ruffian held himself in stout and upright dignity.

"Two bottles of your finest whiskey, for a start, Miss Henry," the man said in a deep and commanding voice.

Martha issued a demand to fill the request without removing her eye from the man and his cohorts. "You appear to have been long on the trail. Will you desire rooms and baths?"

"We do require rooms. Be up to the boys whether or not they choose a bath. For now, I'll settle only for the whiskey."

"I provided an introduction," Martha said icily, "Would you kindly do the same?"

"The man removed a wide-brimmed black hat with a low crown and nodded a head still thick with white hair. "My name is Stu Graybow. The gent in my group is David Hathcoat. The names of the others matter only to me."

After introducing himself and the dandy, Graybow had paused as if to suggest the significance of their names. It took a matter of seconds, but the significance dawned on a woman keen for reading news accounts on a daily basis. What she read, she seldom forgot.

"I know who you are," Martha said before turning a resentful eye on Hathcoat. "Both of you."

"And I know of you, Miss Henry, thanks to the writings of Mr. Hathcoat."

Martha turned a full scowl on Hathcoat. "His ridiculous accounts did me no kindness," she hissed.

Hathcoat turned from her glare to arrogantly look elsewhere, and Graybow chuckled without apparent humor.

"Still yet, it is his accounting that brought me this far for no other reason than to make your acquaintance."

A curiosity calmed her ire just enough to let her look back to Graybow. "And what could possibly be your intent to do so?"

"To give you an opportunity to once again grace the pages of an adventure to be penned by Mr. Hathcoat."

* * * *

The woman's tone of superiority, if not outright repulsion, might have given offense to Graybow at an earlier age. For now, he willingly allowed the madam her haughty reservations. His hired guns had moved to the ornate bar and Hathcoat selected a table just out of earshot from where Graybow and the proprietor shared a smaller table for two.

"What you propose, Mr. Graybow, is utterly preposterous," Martha replied with her nose all but pointed to the ceiling.

"Not the way I see it, and not the way I hope to make you see it, Miss Henry," Graybow said, doing his best not to resort to the tendency of raising his voice. "You fail to realize this has all been one great and bound adventure. It started with the killing of your beau Dallas Babb by Clay Bardoe, and then the killing of Bardoe by CB Wooly, and continued by my killing of CB Wooly, but it is not over. Given the opportunity, Wooly's deputy, Floyd Danner, will try to kill me. He will be given the opportunity, but I will see him dead. What started with Babb, will end with Danner, and you have the opportunity to see it all take place."

Graybow noted a faint spark of interest in the madam's eyes, and he gave her a moment to gnaw on his words before continuing. "Mr. Hathcoat will, of course, memorialize the great event in writing, and this time…he will portray you with words of your choosing."

Graybow sat silently in his typically ramrod straight fashion and waited for Martha's response. When she made up her mind to speak, she took the topic in a direction Graybow did not anticipate.

"Mr. Graybow, out of curiosity, how will you have Mr. Hathcoat memorialize the manner in which you killed CB Wooly?"

He might have been angered at the question, had it not been high-time someone asked it. He'd awaited the question from Hathcoat, but knew the less than courageous author struggled with how to pose it. Graybow thought courage a fine trait in anyone and found it particularly attractive in this woman. Although, until now, no one presented him with this challenge. He'd decided early on how he would respond.

"I'm an old Indian fighter, Miss Henry. As such, I learned as a mere lad to take whatever means available to kill an opponent. If situation allows, and the one you intend to kill deserves honor, then kill in an honorable fashion. CB Wooly did not deserve any better than being shot in the back like a mangy and stray dog. And, that, is how Hathcoat will tell it."

His answer brought a near smile to the madam's lips, and her eyes did seem to soften just a bit when she addressed him again. "So, I accompany you to your ranch in No-Man's Land, where I'm presented the opportunity to witness the closing of this great saga. I do find merit in that, Mr. Graybow, for I hold an affinity for high and violent drama. But, I must finally ask, why is it you desire me to accompany you?"

Graybow fought back the urge for a premature smile of victory. "You are already part of what you call a saga. When I make my reentry in Beaver City, I want you on my arm. A man with a handsome and famous woman at his side, is already one-up on those who might deem him…less than what he truly is."

With a nod of her well-kept head, Martha Henry declared, "I will need but two days to get my affairs in order."

Graybow raised his glass to the madam and awarded himself with a smile.

CHAPTER FOUR

Tamed and Dignified

With another two days on the road since recruiting Zed Martin, Danner reined his horse to a halt, not sure his eyes were sending a proper message to his brain. "What the hell?" He said mostly to himself, but loud enough the others heard it as well.

"Hell, if I know," Walt responded.

"Why I's knows," Abe joined in, "It's sho-nough a naked white man!"

"An old naked white man," Zed inserted.

"Old, naked, white, and a giant of a man," Danner confirmed, smug with the fact his eyes did not deceive him. "But still…what the hell?"

"Why not we ride on up and inquire?" Walt asked.

Danner turned a perturbed glare on Walt. "Well, I reckon that is what we'll be doing, Walt. As if we have any other choice? See-uns how we ought not turn back the direction we came just because a naked man is walking our way down the middle of the road."

Walt shrugged his shoulders and replied, "Thought you might be in need of my opinion once again, Floyd."

"Do you intentionally try to annoy me, Walt?"

"Keeps my mind off drinking, Floyd,"

Danner exhaled a disgusted grunt and nudged his horse forward. He reined to a stop again within shouting distance of the stranger blocking their progression.

"Why are you walking down this road naked?" He called out.

"'Cause I ain't got no damned clothes no more, you stupid son of a bitch!" The much older man shouted back. "I would be riding down this road naked, but I got no damned horse no more either, you stupid son of a bitch!"

"He seems to be of ill-temperament," Danner informed his party.

"Seems he has reason to be," Walt affirmed.

Danner held his place in the road until the naked man stomped up and stopped a respectful distance to their front.

"You got anymore stupid damn questions?" The man asked Danner.

Danner took a moment to study the man with shoulder length hair, and a beard that hung nearly to his nipples, hair and beard looked the grayish color of fog, and both appeared well in need of a washing. The face loomed darkly tanned and deeply creased, the large hands sun-darkened as well, looked gnarled but powerful. The rest of the body glowed pallid white.

"I would like to know," Danner grinned, "Why you are absent of both 'damned' clothes and 'damned' horse."

The older and mountainous man did not return the grin. "Because a passel of damned highway men deprived me of both my clothes and horse and even my damned weaponry. I do so hope you are men of better quality that might assist me in recovering my damned possessions. But if you, too, be highway men, then you are shat out of luck because I have given all I have to damn give."

"We are not thieves," Danner chuckled, "We are, instead, the kind willing to help, depending on your calculation of a passel."

"A passel is three," the old man bellowed. "Any damned fool knows that."

"That depends on your schoolin'," Danner smiled. "Three is one less than a few, the way I was taught to cipher."

"Good God almighty," Hound hollered out, "Someone up front throw the man down a duster."

"Glad you cared to join in, Hound," Danner laughed over his shoulder. "I would offer the gent my slicker, but it would barely cover his considerable private regions."

"I's loan him use of mine's," Abe said as he pulled forward to hand down a union cavalry overcoat.

"Never thought I'd be thanking a damned nigra, but thank you nigra," the naked man said before hurriedly donning the coat.

"The man's name is, Abe," Danner barked. "I would appreciate you addressing him as such. And by the way, what do we call you?"

The man looked from Abe to Danner and then back to Abe. "I meant no offense, Abe. Thank you for use of your damned coat. Color of a man's skin do not make a shat to me. I call a goat a goat because that is what my damned pappy taught me to call a goat. I call a nigra a nigra 'cause he taught me that name as well."

Abe smiled down at the man, "We's all learned from our pappies. Both da good and da bad."

The man nodded his agreement and looked back to Danner. "My official name is Colonel Isaiah M. Stokes. The M. stands for Matthew. But you can call me the damn name given to me by Kit Carson his own damned self, that name being, Sawbuck Sam. He started in calling me that when he saw me shoot a no-account who bilked me out of ten bucks. The no-accounts that just robbed me not two miles back, took from me three times that amount. With a little help, I intend to shoot them as damn well."

"Well, uh, Sawbuck Sam, if my partners be in agreement…" Danner started.

"Most folk shorten it to just Sawbuck."

"All right, Sawbuck, if my partners be in agreement, we will pursue the men who robbed you. We'll try to get back your belongings, but we'll not be shooting them unless they give us no other choice. If they surrender, we'll expect you to deliver them to the nearest lawman."

"Can we hang the damned bastards? Horse thieving is a damned hanging offense."

"Once found guilty by judge or jury, Sawbuck. None of us are either, and neither are you."

"Well, damn it, guess I will have to do it your way."

Danner nodded and turned to his four, "Boys, anyone object to this temporary delaying of our true objective?"

None did. Danner turned his horse to face Hound. "Hound, you have the biggest and strongest horse. Do you mind if Sawbuck here crawls up behind on you on ol' Moonshine?"

Hound pondered the question for long seconds before finally scowling and saying, "Only if Sawbuck does not mind pulling that coat real tight against his damn front parts that will be rubbing against my damn hind parts."

* * * *

Hound with his passenger pulled ahead to track the thieves, and Danner found it amusing that Abe seemed to take a true interest in the newest member of their party. He thought it could have been for no other reason than Abe probably seldom, if ever, encountered a man even bigger than himself. The truth came to light when Abe pulled alongside the men riding two up and addressed Sawbuck.

"Col'nel Sawbuck, what army did you's serve with?"

It turned out to be the lofty title that intrigued the former soldier.

"Ain't never been officially a member of no man's army. I was awarded my damn honorary rank for serving as a scout for more than one general. Served for a while for ol' Georgy Custer, but me and that damned scoundrel never seen eye to eye. Good thing, or I would now be butchered as well."

"General George Armstrong Custer? Lordy, Lordy, I's sho would a like to meet that man!"

"No, you would not, Abe. The feller held most folk in low esteem, but particularly looked down upon nig…uh, darkies."

"Most high and mighty natcha'ally that way. Don't makes him a bad man all in all."

"Oh, he was a bad man for a lot of damned reasons. Now, the last damn general I scouted for is one damn fine man, General Ranald Mackenzie. I helped him find that murderous demon Quanah Parker. Damn sure did."

"Quanah Parker?" Abe yelped. "Lordy, Lordy!"

"Floyd!" Hound interrupted Abe's astonishment, "They turned off the road here, and up that trail. I would bet they are looking for a place to camp for the evening."

"I'm betting they are divvying-up my damned thirty bucks," Sawbuck bellowed.

"Okay, boys," Floyd called out to the others, "Ready your iron. Hound, you and I will scout ahead, taking it slow and easy."

* * * *

"Good Lord, Floyd," Hound whispered, "those three are between hay and grass. Just mere boys."

"Yup, look to be just sprouts for sure, but old enough to rob a man, Hound. So, old enough to answer for it."

Danner and Hound left the others behind to go forward alone after the spotting of nearly steaming horse turds. Now they'd crept to within a hundred yards of the three highwaymen preparing their evening camp. They were indeed youngsters. A fact that certainly did not prevent them from being dangerous all the same.

Danner and Hound put together a plan, which involved Hound staying to keep eyes on the boys. Danner went back for the others. Within an hour, the three outlaws were surrounded, but did not yet know as much.

The young men in the camp by now started a fire and settled around it. Two pulled up logs and set upright. The third reclined with his head and shoulders against his saddle. Zed positioned himself to take charge of the four tethered horses. Floyd would announce their presence, and Walt knelt behind a sturdy tree, ready to perform a specific action.

Danner stepped into the clearing, within fifty feet of the campfire, with Colts at the ready. "Throw up your hands boys!" He thundered, "We have you surrounded!"

The ensuing response did not surprise Floyd. He'd discussed it with the others and assumed correctly that youthfulness alone would more than likely produce a rash and rambunctious reaction. One of the boys sitting a log reached for a gun on his belt, the one resting against the saddle rolled for a nearby Winchester. The third one froze in place.

Walt singularly, as planned, performed magnificently. Two of three rounds fired went into the ground at the seated man's feet, discouraging him from tugging free the pistol from his belt. The third round, fired in less than a bird's wink, knocked the Winchester out of the other's reach.

Floyd rushed in quickly to point his Colts into the faces of the two who'd chosen resistance. Hound and Abe bounded in from opposite directions, preventing any further opportunity for fight or flight.

The boy who'd tried for the Winchester, cautiously pushed to his feet, but did nothing to disguise blatant arrogance. "What the hell you fellers doing? We ain't gone and done nothing wrong."

Then Sawbuck Sam stomped into the clearing, with huge hands extended for the mouthy thief. Walt blocked his advance with Abe's assistance.

"Now holt on, Col'nel, we gots 'em under control."

Floyd grinned at the standing boy. "Ain't gone and done nothing wrong except thieving and horse stealing."

"Don't know what the hell you are talking about," the boy snarled. "We ain't never seen that ol' man in our life. Have we, Justin?"

The boy on the log that tried to pull iron displayed the same insolent attitude, "I ain't never seen the ol' bastard before. Have you, Marcus?"

The other young man perched on a log, the only one who didn't go for a gun, shot a nervous glance to the standing boy and then another at the one to his side before dropping his head and mumbling. "No...don't think so."

Danner stepped up to Marcus and used the barrel of one of the Colts' to gently lift the boy's head. "Lying does not seem to come as easily for you as it does your partners in evil doing." This one's eyes were all but tearing up.

"Leave him be, you son of a bitch!" The standing kid bellowed as he bolted toward Danner. Before Danner could react to the sudden movement, Abe grabbed the boy by an arm and used his momentum to swing him around and sit him down on his ass.

Danner looked down at the young thief and grinned yet again. "We are now acquainted with Justin and Marcus here. How shall we address you?"

"My name ain't none of your business you son of a..."

Abe planted one of his government issue boots in the boy's chest to pin him to the ground. "You ain'ts gonna use fowl words on my friend, Floyd, Suckl'n. Best get to sayin' you name." Abe applied increasing pressure on the pinned kid's chest until receiving the desired effect.

"Tommy!" The boy gasped. "My name is, Tommy."

"Whys I's awfully glad to meets you, Tommy," Abe said good naturedly before reaching down and effortlessly jerking Tommy to his feet.

"What you gonna do with us?" Marcus asked with a tremor in his voice. "You gonna hang us?"

"Hobble your lip, Marcus," Tommy growled.

"Young Tommy, we will be giving the orders from this point forward," Danner said before addressing Marcus's question. "No, Marcus, not going to be any hangings here and now. This man you robbed, and you can call him Colonel Sawbuck, has agreed to take you boys to the law. What happens to you then, I can't say."

Floyd took the two steps that put him face to face with Tommy. "Appearing to be the boss man of this gang of thieves, you set about getting the Colonel's clothing."

Tommy did just that, but only after having a cavalry boot applied sideways to his narrow ass.

* * * *

Abe's dandy shotgun proved as handy as the boots on his feet. Within thirty minutes time he'd provided five fat rabbits for the evening meal. Danner felt it best to tie the hands of Tommy and Justin behind their backs. Now, all sat around the campfire enjoying chunks of roasted rabbit. Abe took it on himself to hand feed the bound boys, while Sawbuck Sam entertained with tales from his trapping, scouting, and Indian fighting past.

"Nowadays, damn white folk, all tamed and dignified in these damn parts, consider their elders scalping Indians as an act of savagery. But scalp them, we damn sure did. They did it to us, and we did it right back to them. Nothing gives more damn satisfaction than taking the damned scalp of a damned enemy that did you a grievous wrong."

Danner just couldn't help but feel a sorrow for all three of their captives, but his heart really went out for the boy, Marcus. The youngster, who confessed to be only sixteen, paid close attention to the ramblings of the old man, and clearly quaked at all mentioning of the ways and means the old timer had witnessed and dispensed death.

Sawbuck waded knee deep into a yarn of how he once took on three Comanche warriors all by his lonesome, when suddenly the outlaw Tommy spat out a chunk of rabbit, Abe so graciously provided.

"Why you old windbag!" The gang leader hissed. "All this talk about bravery and fighting skills, and back yonder, up on that road, you quivered like an old woman at the point of our guns!"

Danner expected to pull Sawbuck off the blatant young fool, but the old man did no more than give the youth a mighty nasty look. Still, Tommy's accusation served to bring the telling of Sawbuck's many adventures to a close.

Shortly thereafter, the ancient Indian fighter struggled to his feet and threw his arms over his head to emit a long, harsh yawn. "Well, boys, I will now take my damned leave for the evening. Never liked camping in company. I have always been plagued with terrible damned night gasses, and hate to embarrass myself and offend others with the damned awful odors of my affliction. I will be back early in the morn to take charge of these young ruffians."

Danner's group set about preparing their prisoners and themselves for the night when Walt pulled Danner aside.

"You think it wise, Floyd, that we burden ol' Sawbuck with the responsibility of seeing these boys to justice?"

"Wise, Walt? Hell, I never claimed to hold an ounce of wisdom. Do you not think him up to the task?" Danner scowled.

"Do not know that he is, and do not know that he isn't. Just got a bad feeling about it, Floyd."

"Well, can you do me the privilege of better explaining your bad feeling, Walt?"

Walt Tabor scuffed the ground with his brogans a long moment before responding, "Not really. Just a…bad feeling. Probably nothing."

"If it turns out to be something rather than nothing, Walt, feel free to burden me with it," Danner said before walking away to fetch his bedroll.

* * * *

The three boys sat in their saddles with hands bound to the saddle horns. All three horses were tied in a line one to the other. Tommy scowled, Justin sulked, and Marcus looked about with wide eyes displaying what appeared to be dread and fear. Sawbuck Sam also sat his horse, holding the rope to the first horse in line, which held the scowling, and still arrogant Tommy.

Danner and his men were mounted as well. The sun barely peaked above the horizon when Danner tipped his hat at Sawbuck. "Guess we will be on our way, Sawbuck, and you on yours."

"We never got around to discussing where it is you damn fellers are headed, but where ever it may be, I wish you God's speed," Sawbuck responded with a returning tip of the wide and battered brim of his misshapen hat.

Danner then looked from one tied boy to the other, and said to all in general, "I hope justice is firm, but kind to you three."

"I hope you tumble into a den of rattlesnakes," Tommy grumbled.

Danner took a moment to consider the journey ahead, and could not help but chuckle. "Boy, you might not have to wish too hard for that to in fact come true."

Danner turned his Paint south to the cacophony of his men saying their goodbyes to Sawbuck, and him spouting his damn goodbyes in turn. On this morning, spring tried its best to put winter to past, and it promised a mild day for traversing the rugged terrain of the southeastern region of the Oklahoma Territory. With any luck, by nightfall, Danner and his company of fine men, and Walt Tabor, would find themselves on the plains of northern Texas.

* * * *

Marcus Potts did his best to keep tears from filling his eyes. He'd not been taught by his fine ol' mama to steal from others. Remaining at her side on the farm back on the North Canadian River, like she'd begged him to do, would not have put him in cahoots with sorts like

Tommy Ring and Justin Adair. Marcus's saddlebags held a letter he'd started for his mama. A foreboding dread signaled it a letter never to be completed, much less sent.

Marcus watched with sickening anticipation as Tommy struggled at the rope binding his hands. He wished the old man would notice the attempts Tommy made, for nothing good would come of Tommy freeing his hands. He thought to call out to Colonel Sawbuck, but anticipated maybe sharing a jail cell with Tommy, and did not wish to endure his wrath. They made it barely a mile north on the main north, south route when Tommy accomplished his deed, and flung himself from the back of his horse.

The sound of Tommy's booted feet hitting the ground prompted the old man to first turn in the saddle, and then wheel his horse about. It appeared to Marcus that Tommy intended to rush Sawbuck, but changed his mind as the elder man tugged some kind of ancient buffalo rifle from a buckskin scabbard. Tommy instead bolted across the small clearing for cover in the nearby woods.

"I will be damned boy," Sawbuck thundered, "if you ain't just given me a reason I long for!"

Marcus, along with Justin, screamed objections as Sawbuck brought the rifle to his shoulder and took aim.

* * * *

The only sound not being produced by nature came from the lips of Zed Martin in the form of a whistle. Zed whistled often and whistled well. Danner easily recognized the tune as Stephen C. Foster's *Beautiful Dreamer.* A troop of men could do worse than having an accomplished noise maker. Such helped one to cope with the monotony of riding a horse at a walk. Danner occupied his time trying to put the exact words with the tune, when suddenly another noise, echoing like distant thunder, shoved the merriment of whistling aside.

"That's rifle fire," Walt called out.

"Lordy, Lordy," Abe followed, "I's knows a .50-70 Sharps when I's hears one!"

"Damnation!" Danner bellowed. Sawbuck Sam carried a .50-70 Sharps. Before he could turn his horse and get her into a gallop, two-more shots rang out in quick procession. Danner didn't look back, but heard the pounding hoof beats of his partners joining in pursuit. He calculated that no more than a three-mile span stretched between his party and the other. His mind raced nearly as fast as his horse on the possible meaning of three shots fired from the powerful Sharps rifle. Maybe Sawbuck had shot as a warning or a call for help. If that turned up not the case, Danner dreaded what waited ahead.

His dread turned to confirmation of calamity when he spotted two spooked and rider less horses headed their way. These horses turned aside and bolted into the woods as the five riders thundered toward them, but not before Danner recognized them as being the horses of Tommy and Marcus. A half a mile further along, He spotted Justin's horse grazing off the side of the roadway. Danner's morning coffee turned sour in his gut and fought its way up his piping.

At little less than a hundred yards away, Danner observed three figures lying on the ground. He eased his horse to first a canter, and then a trot. He didn't care to hasten upon a scene he'd most assuredly helped paint. Abe and Hound barreled on past. Walt and Zed pulled alongside and matched Danner's pace. The three did not make eye contact or mutter a word. Up ahead, he watched Abe and Hound jump from their horses and run to the downed boys. Danner watched Hound remove his hat and fling it to the ground, and Abe bury his head in his hands. Danner, Walt, and Zed were fifty feet out when Abe turned and hollered in their direction.

"Lordy, Lordy, good God almighty, he done wents and scalped two of 'ems!"

Danner stopped his Paint and slowly turned her to face the opposite direction. Zed kept going, but Walt reined his horse to a stop as well, but didn't turn to face Danner. From where he sat motionlessly, Danner could hear his men discussing their find in all forms of foul language. He did not turn to face Walt, but still forced words to his lips.

"Was this the bad feeling you could not express?"

"I fear it might well have been such."

"And whom do you hold at blame?"

Walt moved his horse back and around to face Danner head on.

"I hold at blame that old son of bitch Sawbuck Sam. No one else took part in this. Not me. Not our friends yonder. And damn sure not you."

Danner took in a deep breath and held it. When he had to, he released it to the point of slumping in his saddle.

"Floyd," Walt said forcibly, "Don't let them see you like this. It is a grave and dangerous matter that awaits us. Like it or not, they look to you for both strength and guidance...and so do I. You are the closest thing we have to a CB Wooly or a Clay Bardoe."

Danner pulled in another deep breath and straightened in the saddle just as Zed ran up and shouted up to him. "What we going to do, Floyd? We going after that old bastard?"

"Zed, first we're going to bury them boys. Then we are setting out to undertake the...grave and dangerous matter that awaits us. For the time being, Sawbuck Sam will only be pursued by the good Lord himself."

"Okay, Floyd," Zed nodded, "I will see to the digging."

After Zed took off in a run, Danner looked Walt hard in the eyes.

"Walt Tabor, I do not know what to think about you…or me, as far as that goes."

"I got me figured out, Floyd. I'm a drunk with a tendency toward cowardliness. Now, you need only come to terms with your own self."

* * * *

Zed and Abe chipped away at the rocky ground while Hound wrangled up the boys' horses. Danner and Walt went through their pockets for anything that might provide full names. Walt had made a good point minutes earlier.

"These youngsters got kin out there somewhere. Most likely mothers and fathers that would want to know of their passing."

It fell to Danner to go through the pockets of the kid Marcus. The fact Sawbuck failed to disgrace this one by letting him keep his scalp, sat right with Danner. Should he ever once again cross paths with the savage old scout, he'd keep this in mind in choosing the manner in which to kill him.

No documents were found on any of the three, and Danner and Walt sat about lending a hand to the digging. They toiled alongside Zed and Abe just long enough to work up a sweat when Hound rode in with the three horses in tow.

"Zed, if you and Abe would rather go through those saddle bags for documents or correspondence, Walt and I will keep at this task," Floyd offered.

Zed stood upright to stretch his back and wipe sweat from his brow with his abused old hat before looking over to Abe. "Do tell, Abe, can you read?"

"Nope. Sho can not."

"Why, hell, me neither. Floyd, you and Walt might's well leave us to what we can do."

Danner nodded and motioned Walt to follow.

"What do you intend for these horses, Floyd," Hound asked, "They ain't worth driving along with us."

Floyd removed his hat and scratched at his thick head of hair before coming up with an answer. "Hobble them here, Hound, and pen a notice to attach that explains the awful thing Sawbuck Sam did to these young-uns."

"Now that is a powerful smart thing to do," Danner heard Zed say to Abe.

"That be the reason he the boss man," Abe returned. "It takes smarts to be's a boss man."

Walt offered Danner a wink before both men took to going through the saddle bags on the over-used horses. They were not long into the task, when Walt called out to Danner.

"I found a partially written letter from the Marcus kid to his mother."

"Go ahead and read it out loud," Danner said before calling and motioning the others to draw near.

"The hand writing has a lot to be desired, but I can try to decipher it."

Walt held the tattered piece of paper up to take advantage of the mid-morning sun and scowled in an apparent attempt to make out the words. "My dear and loving mama, I find myself returning from Texas and in the company of a couple of hard sorts named Tommy and Justin. I hope to part company with them when I can do so without giving offense. They are not the...something I can't make out...that you would wish me to partner with. I been from home long enough to know home is where I best be and stay. I have seen enough of the world to see nothing as sweet as home. I did see a site of such things you warned of by a man traveling west near…looks like Shamrock? Anyway, it is in Texas…of an Indian unlike the Chickasaws of home. He rode a large, black stallion and sported guns and silver like such…"

Walt stopped and looked up wide-eyed at the others. "Can it possibly be so?"

"Read on, Walt," Danner mumbled, feeling a snake-like squirming in his innards.

"…dressed all in black with fine boots…holding a likeness of our sweet Jesus on the cross…"

"The Apache," Danner spat.

"The killin' Apache?" Zed asked, "but I thought we would be lookin' for him up in the New Mexico territory."

"I did to," Danner nodded.

"But why in tarnation would he be…" Hound started.

"Shamrock," Zed interrupted, "That is near a two-day ride from the cabin where I found Laughing Billy."

Danner stood silently and listened to his men hash-out their thoughts and assumptions on the matter. He took what he heard to form his own opinion.

"Our intended job seems to have now grown yet more difficult and dangerous as well. The Apache and Bemo are joining forces yet again." Danner let a few obscenities fly before offering words of any true value. "Let's get them boys in the ground. We need to find them two killers…before they find us."

CHAPTER FIVE

That it Is

His years of travel spreading mayhem by justly killing the unjust, and a few others as well, left little that confounded or intrigued the Apache. The site before him, however, counted as an exception. Laughing Billy Bemo sat perched upon a corral railing beside the shoddy cabin staring down at the very spectacle confounding and intriguing the Apache. Without looking up, Bemo, waived him in. Thinking he'd ridden this far without being noticed by the buckskin-clad killer gave the Apache pause. A man who lost his instinct for survival would not serve his purposes. Relieved that Bemo knew of his presence, without seeming to do so, heartened the Apache. For that which he intended, guile would prove a valuable characteristic in an accomplice.

The two women sitting on the ground tied back to back, and gagged, looked far from playing out against their restraints. Muffled sounds of bitter discontent spewed from the mouths of women in tattered clothing with hair a mess.

The Apache cocked his head to study the peculiar scene, but held his tongue.

"Bitches done been at it for going on an hour this time, and still full of bile and hatred," Bemo chuckled without conviction. "But done wore my ass out…How you be, Indian?"

"I am quite well white-man, but you, on the other hand, look worse for the wear."

"You ever get an idea, John Paul, you thought was a grand one, but ended up chapping your cheeks?" Bemo giggled.

"I cannot recall such," the Apache concluded.

"If you have a desire to own a couple of white women, I would let these go for near nothin'. You can try 'em out first if you be interested, but I warn you to keep them tied."

If the Apache, unlike the weary man before him, ever considered the luxury of laughter, this would be the time. Although amused, laughter held no place in his life.

"I would purchase them only as kindling for fire," the Apache grimaced.

Two sets of angry eyes turned upon him and vicious and muted curses were leveled against him.

"Rabid, that is what they are, John Paul. Do not draw close enough for them to bite or scratch, or you, too, will soon foam at the mouth." Bemo, seemed to actually find humor in his observation and warning. "By the by, what the hell are you doing here?"

"You told me where I could find you, should I ever care to find you. I am here now because in fact I cared to find you."

"And you once told me that we are lightening and fire and that lightening and fire should never clash because neither would win," Bemo hee-hawed. "So, I hope you didn't come here in hopes of clashing."

"Why would I intend to do you harm?" The Apache scowled.

"There be a hefty bounty on my head," Bemo giggled.

"You insult my dignity suggesting I would stoop as low as to collect a bounty. I assure you, that is not my intention."

"Then what do you intend, In'jun?"

"I intend to be the hunter instead of the hunted. Will you hunt with me, Laughing Billy?"

"Let me grab some belongings and saddle my horse."

"Do you not care what it is we are hunting?"

"Are we hunting away from this place right here where we stand?"

"Most assuredly so."

"That be all I need to hear. Give me ten minutes," Bemo beamed as he sprung from the rail.

"Simply out of curiosity, what shall you do with these two?" The Apache asked with a nod toward the women.

"The coyotes can have them. Be damned if I will get close enough to touch either ever again." Bemo sprinted for the cabin with an outpouring of joyous laughter.

The Apache nudged his stallion threatening close to the bound women and stared down upon them with disgust. "If either of you witches live long enough, men will be riding here. If you tell them where they can find us, they just might kill Laughing Billy, and perhaps even me, but that is unlikely. But if so, the despicable misery you will no doubt suffer will be revenged. Do you care to know our destination?"

Two soiled faces crowned with tousled messes of hair nodded bitterly in unison.

* * * *

Sawbuck Sam had stood deep in the woods and watched Danner and his boys clean up the damned mess. He'd made a life of watching without being seen. He did not fault the group for doing what they did. They didn't live in that time in which you left your enemies as an example for others who might decide to do you grievous harm.

Had he his way, he'd never encountered the three boys, or been subject to their ridicule. They stripped him bare like a damn new born babe, and practically made him beg for his life. Over a long life of riding the plains, Sam begged for as much before, knowing to plead for life one moment, would allow for others in which to extract revenge. Revenge, as revenge is reputed, delivered satisfaction. Still, Sam wished it not necessary.

His first bullet took down the mean-mouthed youth but didn't kill him. He writhed on the ground like a snake stomped in its middle parts. Sam left him to do such, and trained his rifle on the one called Justin. The powerful round knocked the boy from the saddle, and he twitched a moment or two while hanging suspended from his saddle horn. Sam grabbed the reins of the third boy's horse to calm him, and then untied the kid's hands, ordering him to dismount. This one, going by Marcus, deserved mercy. Sam's bullet went straight to the heart. Sam allowed him to go unmolested. Should this one have chosen another turn in the road, he'd likely grown into an almost decent man.

He drug Justin's remains alongside the still conscious Tommy, whose nasty tongue now turned to begging for mercy and evoking the name of Jesus. Sam made Tommy watch as he removed Justin's scalp. Sam made a show of slowly reaching to grasp the hair atop Tommy's head.

"No, mister! Please mister! In the name of Jesus, mister...have mercy!"

"One who shows no damned mercy," Sam said solemnly, "Gets no damned mercy in turn, son."

He scalped the boy, slowly, while breath still pulled and pushed from his worthless lungs.

Sam spent little damned time with the man Danner, but he knew his type. If given a chance, his type would make Sam's type pay for a perceived injustice. Sawbuck Sam knew of only one way to make sure that did not happen. When Danner's damn party pulled away from the makeshift graves, Sam followed at a safe distance. He'd made a life of following and watching without being seen.

* * * *

"Makes sense to me, I guess," Bemo laughed. "About as much sense as you ever make with all that fancy talk of yours, JP!" Bemo nearly busted a gut on this one. He knew the Apache didn't like him calling him, "JP," but John Paul took too long to say, and Bemo couldn't pronounce any of the other names he went by. Besides, the two men had once came close to dying together, and would have, had they not helped each other to keep on living.

"So, your dreams tell you that ol' Deputy Floyd Danner is out to hunt us down…"

"I prefer the term vision," The Apache said under his breath.

Bemo tried to pull his horse closer, but his horse, like about every other living thing, to include Bemo, feared the black beast the Apache rode.

"You got your words, JP, and I got mine, and mine ain't fancy. I call it a dream."

The Apache simply shook his head as if trying to dislodge a pesky fly.

"Anyhows and anyways," Bemo cackled, "We plan to hunt him up before he can hunt us down, and we have no damned idea where to even start hunting. Now, that part, is not real clear to me."

"We will hunt him, by bringing him to us."

"You done said that."

"You did not let me explain."

"Well, if you be waiting for a written invitation to do so, you be blamed out of luck, because I do not know how to write."

The Apache emitted a deep guttural grunt, as he often tended to do with Bemo.

"We will lure him to us by traveling to a place we are both well known and feared. News of us being there, will quickly find its way to Danner. He will come to us, and we will be waiting."

"Well now, you could have said that three miles back," Bemo giggled.

Yet another grunt.

"Now do tell, JP, where is this place we is headed?"

"Beaver City."

Bemo reined his horse to a stop. Eventually, the Apache did the same, and turned his stallion to face Bemo. The look on his face resembled that of an uncaring mama staring at an ugly and stupid child.

"Why, hells bells, In'jun, we are certainly not wanted in that place. We might have to kill the whole town by the time Danner even makes it there."

"We have killed before, White Man, and we have done so with great proficiency."

Bemo clucked at his horse to get it going again.

"You know, JP, when you talk plain and simple, you make a hell of a lot of sense."

* * * *

Danner and his men stopped a respectable distance from the parked buckboard and the lone woman. The wagon squatted beneath the weight of furniture and household goods. The woman stood beside the wagon with a Henry rifle held across her shoulder and at the ready.

"Ma'am," Danner called out, removing his hat, "Are you in need of some sort of assistance?"

A bonnet shielded a comely face from the sun's rays, and tufts of nearly raven hair danced with the breeze. "No, sir, just moved aside to let you men by, not wishing to be inconsiderate in blocking your passage."

By the way the woman held the rifle, she clearly considered the possibility of Danner and the others posing a threat, as any lady traveling alone should have the good sense to do. He knew the decent thing would be to pass on by, relieving the young woman of her anxieties, but the face with the deep blue eyes held him in place.

"Ma'am, you can expect no mischief from me or my friends. We are all of sound morals and integrity."

The woman motioned the barrel of her rifle south, "Well, sir, then prove so by continuing on your way."

Danner knew tarrying any longer would only serve to place more worry upon the woman, but a man seldom encountered such beauty anywhere, much less on a desolate stretch of road with so little beauty to behold.

"Ma'am we are on a mission seeking justice, and…"

"Then you are lawmen?"

"Well, Ma'am, me and this feller here," he pointed at Walt Tabor, "We were lawmen but…"

The woman brought the rifle to bare on Danner, "Sir, your insistence on staying instead of going is working me into a worry."

Danner lifted his hands in the air, dropping his hat back on his head in the process of doing so. "Please, Ma'am, my name is Floyd Danner, this feller next to me is…"

"Floyd Danner?" The woman repeated.

"Yes, Ma'am, Floyd Danner, and this feller is…"

"I know that name."

"If you know the name, Ma'am, you know it is not associated with any kind of…"

"Your name has been in a book has it not?"

"Well, yes, it certainly has, but…"

"I read a lot of books. It stands as one of my favorite pastimes. Remind me what book your name was in?"

"Ma'am, I had a mere mention in books written about Marshall CB…"

"Wooly? You are the Floyd Danner that stood beside him when he went up against Clay Bardoe?"

Danner cocked his head, let out a sigh of agitation, and offered the lady his most charming smile. "I wish to answer you, Ma'am, but you are a hard one to sneak a full sentence past."

The woman granted a smile, showing all teeth in place, and nearly bright as snow. "I suppose I am in fact. Be that as it may, how am I to know you did not choose that name to put me at ease?"

"Ma'am," Danner smiled back, "If I had chose to impress you with a name, I would have chosen a more impressive and readily recognizable name."

The woman scrunched her pretty face in consideration, and Danner added, "Besides, I am, as described in those books, nearly as wide as I am short, and you will remember, I hope, the description of this big black hat I wear." Then another thought came to mind, and he called Hound forward. "This here is my friend, Hound Olivo, and this here horse he rides, is Moonshine."

The woman let go an even lovelier smile and lowered the Henry. "He is as pretty as I imagined."

"In that Hound here had no mention in the books, I do assume you refer to ol' Moonshine."

The woman responded with a giggle, serving to make Danner all but giddy. Then she turned, cupped a hand to her mouth, and called toward the woods on the other side of the road. "Come on out, Annie! We have nothing to fear from these men."

Danner turned in the direction the woman shouted and stared unbelievably at a strikingly familiar looking woman coming from the woods carrying yet another Henry cradled in her arms.

"I do declare," he stammered, "she looks just like you."

"That seems the way with twin sisters, Mr. Danner. She is Annie, and I am Fannie. Our sir name is Francis."

Danner feared his eyes might go blind from simply too much combined beauty.

* * * *

"I'm posted at your back, Kid," Pink Corning said in a low and mean grumble.

Being the youngest of the men Stew Graybow hired, and having the last name of Friday, the others took to calling him Kid Friday, or Kid for short. He preferred being called by his given name of Jack, but didn't care enough about it to make a ruckus with the others. As of yet, a pecking order had not been established, and Jack did not know how he'd fair against anyone of the hired guns. All in the group of five bore reputations of killers. If they hadn't, Graybow would not have chosen them, and paid them handsomely.

None of the men, so far, went out of their way to befriend each other. Jack assumed that, like him, they'd not joined with Graybow seeking camaraderie. So, Jack felt more than a little surprised when Pink came to his assistance.

Jack's eyes remained on the man to his front, who'd just offered a grievous insult in the form of a question, but said over his shoulder, "Thanks, Pink." Jack didn't know if the man to his front held alliances within the Peacock Saloon, but it never hurt to have the help of a lookout.

Jack had not so far offered an answer to the man's demeaning question, but chose instead to just stare into his eyes.

"Did you not hear me, boy?" The offending man of considerable size asked through gritted teeth.

Jack glanced down at the Smith and Wesson the man wore in a well-placed slim-jim holster, mere inches from a calm hand resting on the bar.

"I asked," the man persisted, "if your mama knows her baby boy is in a house of ill repute?"

Jack decided it time to offer a response. "Go away and leave me be."

"Do not think I will…So, what are you going to do about it?"

"I am going to kill you with your own gun."

The hand on the bar moved to grip the Smith and Wesson. Jack, at only nineteen, knew that all men who gripped a gun, didn't necessarily intend to pull it, but it didn't really matter. Besides, Jack desired to see twenty. With the speed of youth, he reached within his frock coat and pulled his knife with its twelve-inch blade, and buried it to the hilt in the man's guts, while reaching with his free hand to wrap his fingers on the hand gripping the Smith and Wesson. Jack gave the knife a healthy twist, and the hand beneath his fell limp. Jack brushed it aside, pulled the gun, thrust it to the man's forehead, and pulled the trigger. The force of the bullet sent the man backwards, freeing Jack's knife from his innards.

When no other fool came to the dead man's assistance, Pink placed a supportive hand on Jack's shoulder.

"Damn, Kid Friday," he mumbled, "You sent that man out with a belly ache and not enough brains left to find his way to hell."

Jack sensed he might warm to Pink Corning.

* * * *

Tabor felt some strange sense of jealousy that Floyd first engaged the slender beauty beside the wagon. When Floyd gave his name, and the girl recognized it, the jealousy turned to dread, and Tabor slowly moved his horse back and to the end of the line. When the twin stepped out of the brush, he felt a near emotion of elation that he, too, might exchange pleasantries with a lovely lady, but stark truth out weighted the flimsy emotion.

Once Annie was introduced, Floyd took to pointing out and naming his crew.

Hound Olivo.

Abe Walker.

Zed Martin…

Only then did Floyd seem to notice that Tabor had moved to the back, and their eyes locked on each other for a long and weary moment for Tabor.

"And way back yonder is…"

Tabor broke eye contact, and lowered his head, preparing to duff his hat as did the others. Distance alone would prevent Floyd from hearing the tortured exhale of breath he emitted.

"…Well, that is, uh…John Turner."

Tabor removed his hat for the ladies, and nodded gratefully to Floyd, who did not return a nod. Tabor knew how it irked Floyd Danner to lie.

Floyd once again engaged the twins in easy conversation, and Tabor felt comfortable enough now to move closer, to both hear the exchange, and enjoy a closer view of the two lovelies. Just a look served as a sweet treat for men accustomed to the loneliness of the trail. Tabor observed that Abe, Hound, and Zed seemed about as comfortable in the presence of the ladies as did a condemned man at his own hanging.

"Well, tell me ladies, if you do not mind," Floyd got around to asking, "where is it you are bound?"

Annie seemed a shy one, content to let Fannie do most the talking. A task, Fannie proved most capable of completing. "Do not mind you knowing in the least bit, Mr. Danner. We are making our way to Claude, Texas, where our Aunt Mildred recently departed for her reward in heaven. She left us her home and mercantile, and we intend to grow old there." Fannie paused only for enough time to once again fill her lungs with air. "Where are you gentlemen bound?"

"To Texas as well. We are headed a little east and north of Shamrock in hopes of finding one, if not two, of the men responsible for killing CB Wooly," Floyd said with definitive nods of his head.

"Annie and I were both shocked and gravely saddened by the news of the marshal's demise. I find your pursuit most commendable. Like us, you will soon be turning to take the passage into east Texas. Shamrock is along our intended path."

"That it is," Floyd said, taking on a look Tabor knew all too well.

CHAPTER SIX

Yet Another Pity

Town marshal Ben Minska strolled casually through the front door of the Peacock Saloon holding a double-barreled shotgun alongside his right leg. Three deputies followed him through the door, but not in such a relaxed manner as their boss. The younger men's experience totaled would fall nearly twenty-years shy of Minska's time enforcing the law. If these men had worn badges in the Wichita of several decades' past, they too would be more relaxed by knowing nothing here and now could match the hellacious years of Wichita's earliest days.

Minska stopped well short of the bar to survey the scene before him. A large man with the top of his head missing lay on the floor in front of the bar. The bartender stood at the end of the bar furthest from the corpse. Only a handful of local patrons were scattered throughout the cavernous room. Holding center stage stood a white-bearded man with maybe some half-dozen years of living on Minska. Lined up behind him were five hard-looking types, most apparently desperadoes. At the table closest to the body sat the Madam Martha Henry, nonchalantly reading a newspaper as if a dead man didn't lay sprawled nearly at her feet. Not bothering to meet the bearded man's evil-eyed stare, Minsk moved to stand over the dead man.

"Martha," Minska said with a drawl, "The deceased seems to be wearing John Steeple's clothing, but I cannot rightly tell if that mangled and blood-splattered face belongs to ol' John."

"Ben, it does, indeed, seem to be ol' John," the madam said without looking up from her paper.

Marshal Minska had long grown accustomed to the old whore's arrogant ways. "Well, Martha, how did ol' John come to lose the top of his head and what little brains it corralled?

"I would not know, Ben. I was upstairs and only came down upon hearing the gun shot."

"Uh-hu, I could have assumed as much," Minska chuckled. "Jack," he shouted to the bartender standing a far piece away, "Do you so happen to know anymore than your employer as to how ol' John kept his date with the devil?"

"Busy making my living with my back turned to the saloon, Marshal. Saw not a damned thing."

"Hmmmm," Minska grinned, "Wonder why I somewhat expected that to be the case, Jack?"

The bartender offered only a shrug of his shoulders in response.

Minska slowly turned in place to meet the stare of the haughty man standing in front of his team of henchmen. He held the stare while calmly walking within touching distance of the bearded face.

"Seeming that you are the biggest toad in this puddle, mister," Minska said with an easy grin, "Do you care to impart how ol' John came to be dead there on the floor?"

The older man maintained his mean expression, and replied in a most snide way, "Looks to me that he put his own gun to his head and blew it to hell."

Minska nodded his head and chuckled, "Men who lower themselves to the state of frequenting this establishment have been known to do that from time to time. But that looks to be a knife wound in his gut. Never known a man to stab himself before putting a gun to his head."

"Desperate men sometimes take to desperate actions," the bearded man grumbled.

"Yup, that they do," Minska smiled. Then he let the smile slowly fade away. "You've been in my town now about three days. About time we got acquainted. Tell me, boss man, what name do you go by?"

"My name is Stew Graybow, but you can address me as Mr. Graybow."

Minska had long made his living by remembering the names of the despicable types. "Well, that is going to happen right after you kiss my bony, bare ass."

Bearing an ugly snarl, Graybow took a step that placed him in Minska's face. In a smooth instance, the shotgun came up with both hammers cocked to rest firmly beneath the bearded chin. Behind Graybow, hands went to guns, and behind Minska echoed the sound of his deputies cocking their shotguns.

"Easy boys, easy," Minska said calmly.

"I give the word, and you are a dead man," Graybow grumbled.

"Uh-hu, but you will not give the word. Know how I know that?"

"Do tell," Graybow spat.

"I know, by the accounts I read that you were once a fierce Indian fighter, but I also know that you put bullets in the back of a dying man. CB Wooly was a friend of mine. No finer man ever wore a badge. Somewhere along the line, Stew Graybow, you lost your nerve. You will not do a damned thing right now, because you know you will die right along side of me. In your old age, you have grown too cowardly to die like a man."

"You do not want to push me," Graybow thundered.

"No…I do want to pull you though." Minska used his free hand to grab Graybow's right ear. With the shotgun thrust harder still beneath his chin, Minska started moving backwards. "Back out of here, boys," he called to his deputies.

Graybow cursed every step of the way, but offered no resistance. Once in the doorway, Minska dropped his hand from Graybow's ear. "I will be wiring for federal marshals. They will be here by sundown. I suggest you and your troop of cut throats be long gone by the time they ride in."

* * * *

Abe's use of the newfangled shotgun once again proved a source of hardy eating. Danner and his men, along with the Francis twins sat around a communal campfire and supped on both squirrel and rabbit, while Danner explained to the women their current pursuit of the mysterious Indian and laughing madman.

"I do certainly hope you find and punish those horrible men for what they did to Marshal Wooly, and I wish you each God's protection," Fannie said, and Annie agreed with nods of her head with a furrowed brow of obvious worry.

When all but a few morsels remained untouched, Fannie moved from the fire to their nearby wagon and retrieved a matching set of fiddles.

"Enough of this talk of ugliness done, and that sure to come," she said to Danner, and then directed a smile to Abe, "Such a fine meal deserves a celebration of merriment."

The dim glow of the campfire barely reflected the look on the big man's dark face, expressing to Danner shyness and discomfort of being in the company of two white women. The girls had shown no aversion to the color of his skin, but Danner knew that lines were drawn deep in Abe's thinking of improprieties created by the societal norms of the day. He sat as far as possible from the women, speaking when only spoken to.

The two cowboys, Zed and Hound, didn't sit much closer. Their shyness came from a different source, stemming from their only experience with women being that of mothers, sisters, and whores. Their responses to the girls had come only in nods and shrugs and embarrassed smiles.

Walt Tabor seemed to do his best to ensure that Danner was always between himself and the twins. Danner figured it not shyness that imposed his silence, but a deep dread of impending shame. Danner wanted to pity the man for the burden, but could not find it in himself to do so.

Fannie handed one of the fiddles to Annie and the girls positioned themselves side by side in front of Danner's fidgeting comrades. In unison, their toes started to tap seconds before both ladies exhibited an impressive skill with their musical instruments. They started with the lively "Turkey In The Straw" and kicked it up a notch with "Buffalo Gals," before Fannie lowered her fiddle to allow Annie to play a solo of "My Old Kentucky Home," while Fannie sang with what Danner surely believed to be the voice of an angel.

Before she started the second stanza, Danner accepted the whirlwind whipping about in his innards as that of true and eternal love. He quickly scanned the faces of his men, embarrassed that they might have observed outward signs of the affection he held in his heart for the beautiful Fannie. He relaxed when they seemed not to notice, and felt some sense of relief to find Walt staring at Annie in much the same manner he'd stared at Fannie.

Several tunes later and nearing midnight, the girls put the fiddles away and all started preparing themselves and the camp for slumber. Danner was laying out his bedroll when Walt came up close and spoke in nearly a whisper.

"What plans have you made, Floyd, for parting company with these women?"

"Well, Walt, I have made no such plans. I failed to see it as a priority," he whispered back with a scowl.

"I suggest the sooner we do so, the better. We can assuredly move faster without them, and we need not take chances of putting them in harm's way."

"Walt, the way you were eyeing that young Annie, I thought you might want to prolong parting until absolutely necessary to do so," Danner probed with a grin.

"I did not look at her any more lasciviously than you did her sister," Walt bristled, "Besides, she knows not my true identity, and will harbor only disgust when and if she learns my secret."

Danner knew no better way to respond than offering a nod and a shrug of his shoulders.

"Please consider my advice, Floyd."

"Quite often, Walt," Danner said as he turned back to his bedroll, "you tend to chafe me worse than rain-soaked trousers."

* * * *

Since most the Indians were either dead or starving on reservations, the damned white men had grown too damned at ease on the plains. In Sawbuck Sam's day, no worthwhile, or certainly long-living party of men, would let themselves be snuck upon like Sawbuck had done the Danner party earlier in the evening. He'd practically perched right on top of them, observing all they did, and hearing all they said. Of course, Sawbuck had long ago learned to sneak and hide without being seen as efficiently as any damned Comanche that ever roamed the region.

He'd enjoyed listening to the fine fiddling, and had not yet aged so far that he still did not enjoy the viewing of lovely ladies. But music and lusting had not been the intent of his reconnoitering the party. He wanted to know the true purpose of Danner's journey, and now he knew it. Although Sawbuck's name had not been mentioned, he pegged Danner for the type that would be coming after him once he caught up and dealt with the strange Apache and the laughing man they called Billy. Sawbuck knew of only one way to keep that from happening. He'd somehow have to meet up with the men they sought, before Danner and his men found them. For the time being, until he knew more, Sawbuck would just follow and listen at every chance he got.

* * * *

"Come out of that house now Minska, or we will burn it down around you!"

Marshal Ben Minska jerked upright in his bed a split second before his wife of nearly forty-five years did the same.

"Ben... what in the world..."

He shushed her by placing a hand gently across her mouth. "They are a gang of bad men, Mama. This surely will not end well."

He tugged his wife from the bed and moved her to a corner of the house with a straight shot at the front door. Ignoring her sobs and pleas for clarification, he hurried to gather his hand guns, rifle and shotgun.

"Do you hear me in there, Minska? I will set a match to this shack so help me God!"

"I am coming, Graybow," he shouted back, "Allow me the decency of giving my woman a proper good-bye."

"You got three minutes, you son of a bitch!"

Ida Minska cried loudly as Ben gently pushed her to the floor and arranged his guns all about her. He pressed a pistol into her hand and forced her fingers around the grips. "Mama, once I go out, I will not be coming back in. I am going to do my best to keep them from coming in this house, but if I fail, and they do… you start laying down lead, and do not stop until all guns are empty."

He hugged her tightly and kissed her cheeks and forehead before pushing to his feet.

"Oh, Ben! No, Ben! You must not…"

"You have been a good wife, Ida, and I loved you the most and best I knew how. I do hope to hold you again in heaven."

Minska moved in long strides toward the door with his wife screaming his name.

* * * *

Graybow sat his horse in front of the rural residence with his mounted men arranged to his left and right. The Madam Henry's coach and Hathcoat's buggy were parked on the dirt road to his rear. The woman insisted on sitting close enough to see the town marshal receive his comeuppance.

Minska stepped out the door in his bare feet, wearing only a pair of suspendered trousers and an undershirt. He closed the door firmly behind him, but it did little to muffle his woman's pitiful crying.

"You cared not to come out heeled," Graybow observed.

"Being armed would not do me much good now, would it Graybow?"

"You goddamned right about that," Graybow agreed while loosening a lariat from his saddle.

"I have only one request, Graybow. I know sometime in your long life, you must have held some sense of honor…most men do. I ask now that you give me your solemn oath that no harm will come to my wife."

"I never done harm to a woman in my life, and do not intend to start now. Besides, my beef, is only with you. I give you my word she will suffer no wrong doing."

Minska straightened tall and proud. "Then, do what you come to do. I stand ready to meet my maker."

"Do you care to apologize for calling me a coward before so doing?" Graybow called down from his horse.

"I certainly do not."

Graybow gave the lariat an experienced toss that landed around Minska's shoulders. Graybow used flicks of his wrist to pull-it up and tight around the lawman's neck. He secured the other end around his saddle horn.

"In that case," Graybow grinned, "let me see how long you last at a gallop."

He turned his horse, roughly applied his spurs and jerked the man from his front porch. Just to please his female escort, he first took a fast couple of laps around her coach before directing the horse down the road at a full-blown gallop. His men and the wagons gave pursuit.

* * * *

From the glow of a full moon, Martha Henry had observed Graybow lasso Ben Minska on his front porch. She felt sure at that moment that Graybow intended to simply and boringly hang the marshal. It greatly impressed Martha that, instead, he meant to drag him to death. Such a brutal act spoke of a flair for extracting true vengeance, a virtue that Martha appreciated in men, no matter if of advanced age or not.

The first lap Graybow made around her coach revealed Minska clawing at the rope around his neck. By the second lap, his arms flailed alongside his twisting, tossing, and bouncing body. Martha only followed the galloping horsemen for less than a mile before easing her horses to a trot. The despicable writer of fabricated nonsense had already fallen far behind her in his buggy. For nearly an hour she followed the trail of shredded remnants of Minska's garments.

She topped a small hill in the roadway to find the mounted men sitting their horses in a semi-circle. At their feet, torn and tattered, lay the nearly nude form of Ben Minska. The far end of the rope around his mutilated neck was still secured to Graybow's saddle horn. From what Martha observed, the head would not have long stayed attached to the body.

"I thought you had given up the chase," Graybow called out to her as she brought her coach to a standstill.

"I set my own pace, Graybow," she responded. She well knew by now that it irritated him greatly for her to use his last name without a mister attached, and that she was the only one afforded the slight.

Moments passed with Graybow staring her direction before he loosened the rope from his saddle horn and tossed it to the ground. He turned in his saddle to look to a man on his left and addressed the one the others referred to as Kid.

"Friday, this is all a result of your actions. Had you not killed one man, without my orders to do so, I wouldn't have been forced to kill this one. A spade is attached to the back of Miss Henry's coach. Crawl down and dig the marshal a grave."

Martha's pulse quickened when Kid Friday pulled his horse closer to Graybow's in a most agitated manner.

"And what if I choose not to?" the young man asked in a growl.

"I have only paid you, and the rest of these men, half of what I promised for your services," Graybow growled back. "If you do not do as told, not you, or any of the others around you will receive the balance. I think these men are not the type to let you spoil a sweet deal."

Friday turned to look at his peers, obviously seeking an ally. The man Martha knew only as "Pink," offered the first response.

"Best do it, Kid, and I will give you a hand."

"No, you will not," Graybow barked.

Friday sat silent for only a moment before another in the group said in a stern voice, "Get to it, Kid. I intend to get the rest of my damned money."

Martha watched other heads nod in agreement to the demand. She felt a sense of relief when the younger man dejectedly swung from the saddle and started in her direction. Kid Friday was one damned good-looking young man. Although she harbored a delight for viewing violence, she could imagine better outcomes for this one than being gunned down beneath a glowing moon.

Once Kid Friday busied himself breaking the ground, Graybow dismounted and walked up to stand beside her coach. Martha spoke the first words.

"When Minska held you at gunpoint, I did so wish you would do something dramatic. Of course, I realize, that would have only proved you a fool. Dying was truly your only option. Now, from your actions here tonight, I have learned you are a most wily and shrewd old bastard, which has placed you notches higher in my books."

"In that case," Graybow replied with a nasty snarl, "I will forgive you of both referring to me as old and a bastard."

* * * *

The late night before turned to dawn far too soon for Zed Martin. Although he'd not had even a sip of strong drink, he went about readying his horse as if suffering from a hangover. It surprised him when Hound Olivo approached with a rolled cigarette and handed it in his direction.

"Have a smoke, Zed?"

"Don't mind if I do. Much obliged." Zed took the cigarette and watched curiously as Hound rolled another for himself. When words formed in Zed's mind, he'd never been apt at keeping them there. "You ain't said ten words to me, Hound, since we been on this ride. Why you now offering me a smoke?"

"No sense judging me by words spoken, Zed. I just have little to say."

Zed nodded his head in response and watched as Hound flicked a match to light both cigarettes. He turned his head to watch the women breaking camp in a distance as he pulled the smoke deep into his lungs.

"Hound, which of those girls do you think the prettiest?"

Hound pulled a floppy hat from his head and scratched at matted hair before responding, "Why hell, Zed, their twins. They look just alike."

Zed chuckled at the response before replying, "Yeah, you make a point, Hound. But I prefer the one who does the most talking."

"Guess if I had the luxury of choosing one," Hound said through a plume of smoke, "she would be my choice as well. The other has nearly as much to say as I do. We would never get acquainted."

Zed again expressed a response with laughter. Both men stood silent as they finished their smokes. Again, words came that could not be contained.

"What have we gotten ourselves into here, Hound? I mean in giving chase to the Indian and Bemo?"

Olivo tossed his cigarette to the ground and smothered it with a well-worn boot heal. "Very likely, Zed…dying."

"Kind of strange, Hound, thinking about dying, that is. You know you get to an age where you know all folks do it sooner or later. I was always hoping it would be later than sooner. Kind of thought I might one day have a little ranch my ownself. Maybe even a wife and a few kids as well."

"Not saying you won't be doing that still. Don't mean we're all going to die, but it'd be unusual, considering the types we'll be fighting, that at least a couple of us didn't end up dead."

"Got any advice for me not ending up being one of the couple, Hound?"

"Yup. Just don't get shot, Zed."

Sensing Hound had said all he intended, Zed extended his right hand. Hound took it and gave it a firm shake. Both men then went about their business with a nod and a grim smile.

* * * *

Danner rode up and looked down at the dismounted Walt Tabor.

"This looks like about a good a place as any to spend the night, Floyd."

Danner removed his hat and ran his fingers through sweat soaked hair. Ten hours in the saddle wore him smooth. "Another hour of daylight, but don't think I have another hour in me. I agree with you, Walt, we should call this home for the night."

"We covered a lot of ground today. Those gals stayed right up," Walt said as Danner swung from his saddle."

"That they did, Walt. Guess you now won't mind spending another day on the trail with them?"

"One more long day, Zed says, will put us at the Bemo place. When do you expect we should part company with them, Floyd?"

Danner sensed Walt not so enthused about the parting as he'd been the night before. "I saw you talking with Annie at the water hole earlier in the day," he pried.

"Yeah. She is a fine lady. Easy to talk to," Walt said with a glance over his shoulder to where the women parked their wagon about fifty yards in the distance. He turned back to Danner and pried in turn, "You spent the biggest part of your day riding beside that wagon and chatting like a school-girl with Fannie."

"Yeah," Danner grinned, "She is a fine lady. Easy to talk to."

"You might just meet up with her another day, Floyd."

"I hope to, Walt. And you might just do the same."

"Not likely," Walt sighed.

"When I saw you talking to Annie today, it occurred to me, that if you make a stand with us, like only you could be capable of doing, you'd be nothing less than a hero to anyone of us. Then, you could find young Annie, tell her your real name, and hold your head up high in doing so."

"Don't think I haven't myself considered such, Floyd."

"Well, that's a good thing, Walt.

"Could be. Maybe," Tabor shrugged.

Frustrated at Tabor's inability to fully commit, Danner started leading his horse in the direction of the girls' wagon. He said over his shoulder, "Could be, maybe, that the camp's going to set it ownself up, but doubt it will."

* * * *

Abe didn't fail to bring in the game, and the ladies did a fanciful job of readying it for plates. Tabor laid his utensils on the ground beside him and readied himself for the girls to fetch their fiddles. Hearing them play a final night would be a bitter sweet experience to tuck away with mostly heart wrenching memories of a disappointing past.

His fond expectations turned immediately to dread when Fannie turned from her seat on a log to address Floyd sitting nearby. "Floyd, Annie and I were talking earlier, and we would love to hear about how you came to know CB Wooly and Clay Bardoe. The accounts we read said you had a past with both men, but offered no further explanation."

Floyd removed his big black hat and dropped it at his feet brim up. "Well, now kind ladies, telling that sad story will do nothing for my reputation and will sully not only my abilities, but prove I often lack for good ol' common horse sense."

More than a little interest in Floyd's version caused Tabor to comment without proper consideration. "I too would like to hear that story, Floyd. I only have CB's telling of how you come to meet."

Annie turned wide eyes on Tabor and exclaimed with excitement, "You knew Marshal Wooly too, John Turner? Do tell!"

Chalking up just one more reason to hate himself, Tabor cleared his throat and scratched at his five-day growth of beard. "Oh, uh, Annie, my experience with the marshal…ain't worth the telling."

Annie poised her mouth to say more, but Floyd mercifully once again came to Tabor's rescue, begrudgingly for sure.

"Miss Annie, ol' John's just being humble, but let us hold his story for another time. Now that you ladies have brought that day to mind, my soul aches to purge myself of downright youthful ignorance."

Tabor sighed in relief as he watched Floyd settle into a comfortable position for spinning a yarn. Tabor would be damned before opening his mouth again.

CHAPTER SEVEN

Sin no More

A younger Floyd Danner shook his head to clear his vision. What looked to be two stagecoaches, side by side, made a quick approach toward the fallen limbs he assembled to block the road.

"Damn whiskey," he slurred before slapping his face to sharpen his thinking. He experienced nothing but failure in his miserable existence of the past year, and did not cherish the thought of ruining his first attempt at law-breaking. Why he'd drank nearly half a bottle of whiskey before attempting to rob a stage made no sense, but as of late, Danner seemed to make a good hand at making no sense whatsoever.

With his horse tethered to a tree well off the road, Danner took his position behind a large oak. The single stage, still appearing as two, had no option other than stopping. Danner peaked around the tree to see both the driver and the shotgun-wielding guard craning their necks nervously in all directions and sharing words he could not hear.

After what seemed an eternity, the guard shouted out, "We ain't got all day. Come out with your hands empty or make an attempt to rob us and be damned!"

Danner figured he'd be damned if he did either, so he held his place silently behind the tree. After what seemed long enough for a Baptist minister to deliver a sermon, both men cautiously climbed from the boot of the stage and carefully made their way to the fallen limbs. The guard never released his grip on the shotgun, but did use a free hand to help the driver with the task of clearing the roadway. Only then did Danner pop from concealment to level a Winchester at the armed guard.

"Drop that shotgun or you will be damned," he slurred.

To Danner's surprise, the guard offered no resistance and readily tossed his weapon aside. Not expecting it to be so easy, Danner stood in place until the driver shouted in his direction.

"Do you intend to rob this stage, or are you here to invite us to a social?"

"I in fact intend to rob the stage," Danner admitted with a hearty burp.

"Then get to your deed, man. We don't have all day to stand here with our thumbs in our nether regions."

It would be unusual for the driver not to be in possession of a handgun, but Danner could not see one. "Hey, Whip," he called to the driver using a common moniker for a stage driver, "If you be packing iron, get rid of it."

"I got me one, but I wish you not to shoot me down when I pull it."

"I don't intend on shooting unless forced to do so," Danner shouted.

The driver slowly reached beneath his coat and removed an old Navy Colt. He tossed it aside as if it burned his hand.

Danner nodded his head a number of times before forming his next words. "You, driver, can remove your thumbs from your nether regions and continue clearing that road. Guard, you go back and get the passengers out of the coach. After that, you kick off the strong box."

"You ain't gonna shoot me in the back, are you?" the guard inquired.

In his current condition, Danner could not have hit a barn door while standing in front of it, but didn't think it wise to admit such to the guard. "Just do as told, and no need stands for nobody getting shot no place on their body."

The guard moved to do as told, but never took his eyes off Danner, who tried his level best to keep eyes on both the driver and the guard. More than once he felt a need to shake his head to keep his eyes from crossing. Soon enough a nervous looking man and woman along with two small children vacated the coach. The adults gathered the children in front of them, wrapping them in their arms to calm and protect the youngsters.

"No harm will come to you or your children," Danner called out as he all but staggered toward the stage. The fear on the simply dressed family's faces poked at Danner's conscious, and he fought off both the urge to vomit and the voice in his milky mind telling him to turn and run, letting his dastardly intentions be damned. He jumped and nearly fell over backwards at the sound of the strongbox hitting the hard-packed and rutted roadway.

He used the rifle to motion for the guard to join the family, and then stood swaying on his feet until the driver cleared the path before them. He again used the long barrel to usher the driver up to stand with the others.

"Mister, you do not look too awfully good," the driver observed.

"What I got ain't contagious," Danner grumbled.

"Looks downright drunk to me," the guard mumbled.

"And I have no need of mouthing from you," Danner slurred to the guard, while trying to decide what exactly to do next. He would not have guessed upon the conception of his plan that stage robbing would be such a complicated venture.

"All right, now all I need you to do before I let you get on your way is remove all valuables and toss them down at your feet."

"All I gots is money for my supper tonight," the driver whined.

"I got two bucks to my name," the Guard moaned, "and a pocket watch that belonged to my dear ol' pop, who died of infection in a confederate hospital. Surely you will not deprive me of such a precious possession."

Danner considered clubbing his own self with his own rifle. Who would a' thought it took a special breed to take what they didn't earn? "What about you, sir?" He asked the man standing guard over the children.

"I have cash money. But only enough to establish a home for my family if and when we ever reach Fort Smith."

Danner took a deep breath and exhaled it slowly while rubbing at his face with a trembling hand. "You all load back up and get on out of here."

"Can I toss the strongbox back on top?" the guard asked. "Losing it could cost me my job."

"Do not," Danner growled, "further test my good will and weak heart and lack of ability for stage robbing."

The stage pulled away, and the strongbox remained. Danner stared at it for several long minutes before convincing his legs to carry him off the side of the road to retrieve his horse. Fearing he could not mount, he walked his horse back to the road. Before doing so, he removed the half-bottle of whiskey from his saddle bag and took swigs as he walked.

Back in front of the box, he pulled his revolver and held it beside his leg. "Mr. Strongbox, I fear that you, too, mock me. With the luck I've had, I would be a fool not to bet that you contain nothing more than legal documents intended for a land office." He emptied the revolver of all six rounds before managing to destroy the heavy lock.

Reluctantly, he used the toe of his boot to open the lid, and thought his eyes were surely deceiving him. Stacks of greenbacks filled the box. He shook his head vigorously before taking a second look, and it was indeed heaps of money that he viewed. After letting loose a mighty and victorious whoop, he brought the bottle to his lips and drained the contents. The motion of giving the empty bottle a healthy toss caused Danner to spin in place and fall on his ass. For no telling how long, he lay in the roadway and laughed like a loon. When he could get to his feet, he grabbed fists full of the money and stuffed it into his saddlebags. With the box empty and his saddlebags bulging, he fumbled and stumbled until finally getting into the saddle.

The horse started off at a walk, and the world suddenly turned upside down. Danner grabbed for the saddle horn and missed it. The horse started to spin in circles, or it might have remained at a halt while the trees spun in circles. Either way, Danner left the saddle and landed on the hard ground in a heap. With the air knocked from his lungs, he first fought to breath, but then the upside-down world plunged into soothing darkness.

* * * *

Danner could hear the conversation as clear as day, but his mind did not seem quite ready to respond.

"He didn't get far, Clay."

"That is a fact, CB. About ten or so feet, I'd guess."

"Easiest highway man I have ever pursued, Clay."

"Seems unjust to get paid for taking this one to jail, CB."

Jail. The term brought Danner closer to his senses. Evidently, the shapes starting to take form belonged to that of lawmen.

"Not going to jail," he managed to mumble. "You will not take me alive."

One of the forms broke into laughter.

"You heard the man, Clay. You want to kill him, or should I?"

"You go ahead, CB. Don't care on changing my ways for the likes of this one."

"He is most assuredly the sorry type, and any bullet used would be a waste of good lead. I'm bettin', Clay, all he needs is some more to drink."

Maybe a single minute passed, maybe a passel, Danner did not know because the whiskey still ruled his facilities. That changed when he suddenly felt like his face had been subjected to a downpour of cold rain. He gagged over the amounts of water that worked its way down his throat. Still spitting, sputtering, and gasping, he felt himself being hoisted to his feet. Quick slaps to his jaws, followed by a sound shaking that rattled his teeth, served to somewhat clear both his sight and his mind.

Both men were, of course, taller than Danner, as most men where. The one who held him by his lapels was the stoutest built of the two.

"Are you free enough from the grasp of the devil liquor, boy, to make sense of my words?"

Danner could not yet speak but nodded his head. The man before him released his grip and took a step backwards. Despite his trembling knees, Danner managed to remain upright.

"My name is CB Wooly, and the gentleman at your side, holding the now empty canteen, is Clay Bardoe. We are deputy U.S. marshals, and we suspect you to be a stagecoach robbing son of a bitch."

Danner rubbed at his neck and coughed to clear his throat. "I am certainly no son of a bitch, and most apparently not much of a stagecoach robber to boot."

Wooly chuckled at the response. A glance at Bardoe revealed no apparent signs of amusement. "I do know of you, Mr. Wooly and your partner, Mr. Bardoe. You can expect no resistance from me."

"What is your name, son?" Bardoe asked in a cold, calm manner.

"Floyd Danner, and this was my first attempt ever at wrong doings. I don't ever want to attempt further."

"It seems a wise decision to me, Mr. Danner," Wooly grinned good-naturedly, "because you do not seem to possess the skills for outlawing."

Danner cleared his throat again, "I would just a soon you address me as Floyd. I am not comfortable with men of your notoriety calling me mister."

"As I have heard it said, Clay," Wooly chuckled, "our reputation precedes us."

"So, it does," Bardoe deadpanned.

"Well…Floyd…you committed your crime just a stone's toss from the territory, so we will be taking you to Fort Worth, Texas, to stand trial. That is a fair piece to travel, and we best get on our way."

After Bardoe removed the stolen money from Danner's saddlebags, Wooly helped Danner into the saddle.

"Do you think it necessary that we bind your wrists to the saddle horn, Floyd?" Wooly asked.

"Done said I won't resist, and now I give you my word on it. Besides, I hear told that Mr. Bardoe there can shoot the gonads off a bumblebee in flight. I prefer my gonads to stay intact."

CB Wooly laughed out loud, and Clay Bardoe looked as if he might smile, but didn't.

* * * *

Three riders came into sight on the road some distance ahead. Neither CB nor Clay showed concern. That's what Danner had taken to calling them – CB and Clay. Men could grow quickly familiar with each other after an evening around a campfire and long hours in the saddle on a lonely stretch of road. The night before, sharing a meal, and telling tales, even Clay seemed to grow fond of Danner in the light of the warming fire. Right before they'd turned in, Clay looked Danner straight in the eye and said, "It's truly a pity you saw fit to give into stupidity." Danner had agreed it surely was. Neither lawman thought it necessary to truss him for the night. They had taken him at his word not to flee. He already cared considerably for both lawmen, only regretting that their journey would end with him being tossed in the hoosegow.

When the distance between the approaching parties drew to a space of barely making out characteristics, the three riders ahead reigned to a stop, apparently exchanged words, and then drew up side by side, blocking the road ahead. CB and Clay gave their horses the command of "Whoa," forcing Danner to do the same. At the same time, those on the road ahead pulled rifles from scabbards and laid them across their laps.

"You recognize any of the three?" Clay asked CB.

"Not from this distance." CB responded.

"They pulled their rifles," Danner inserted.

"That they did," Clay answered, "but they ain't aiming them."

CB looked at Danner and gave him a wink. "If I did not have ol' Clay here by my side, I would have mine pulled as well. But mine would be aimed."

"I'll ride ahead. See what they intend," Clay said, as he slowly and inconspicuously pulled his two revolvers from Slim Jim holsters and tucked his filled hands beneath his long coat and opposing armpits. He moved his horse forward with only a verbal command and use of his knees. He did not go so far that Danner couldn't hear the exchanged hollered words.

"Do you men mean us harm?" Clay called out.

One rider pulled slightly ahead of the others. "That fanty-pantsy hat on yo' head, I hears they call it a Montana Peak. Only one man I know of in these parts wears such a new-fangled hat."

"And who would that be?" Clay shouted back.

"I suspect you to be Clay Bardoe, and one of those two's behind you I figure to be CB Wooly."

"Then you suspect and figure right. Do I know who you are?" Clay challenged.

"Not just yet, but you will soon learn, you bastard. You and whichever of those other two be CB Wooly, seen to the hanging of my little brother, Johnny Webb."

Had he not been tense enough to pass milled lumber, Danner would have chuckled when CB removed his hat and waved to signal that he was in fact CB Wooly.

Clay started slowly forward on his horse, and CB did the same before saying to Danner, "You stay here. If they get the best of us, which ain't likely, you flee…and sin no more."

"I remember Johnny Webb," Clay shouted. "He slaughtered an innocent family in the territories. That noose fit him well."

The man out front issued an apparent command to the others, and rifles were raised to the ready.

Clay put the spurs to his mount, and it took off at a gallop as he pulled his guns free from beneath the long coat. CB pulled his rifle and gave pursuit of his partner.

The three men let go with a volley, but Clay charged ahead, holding his fire. Danner could see the men working their levers for yet another volley when, one by one, they fell from their saddles. CB never fired a shot. Clay had taken them by himself...one, two, three.

Danner raced ahead and reached the fallen and withering men as Clay covered them with his Colts while a dismounted CB kicked away their rifles. One downed man clawed at a shoulder, another a thigh, and the third a right arm.

"Damn, Clay," Danner exclaimed, "I always heard you shot to only wound. How could you land your rounds with such accuracy at a gallop?"

"I proved not to be all that accurate," Clay responded calmly while pointing a pistol to the man holding his right arm. "I aimed at his left one."

"Been up to me," CB growled to the wounded men, "You would all be dancing with the devil right now."

CHAPTER EIGHT

Company of Demons

Tabor felt only slightly less impressed with the telling than did the two lovely women. Floyd looked exhausted from recalling the memory. He ended his story with a sigh and pulled the two pearl-handled Colts from his holsters and lifted them in exhibition. "It was these very guns Clay Bardoe used to drop those men from their saddles...I am not worthy to tote them now."

When Floyd dropped his arms to his side, Fannie boldly hooked an arm in the crook of Floyd's arm. "Nonsense! You are, after all, the man who stood by CB Wooly's side in Stillwater and again in Beaver City. That makes you worthy of toting those Colts anytime and anyplace."

"I's didn't know either man, tho' Lordy, Lordy I's likes to have," Abe chimed in, "and I's bettin' they both be proud of you now and wouldn't wants no other mens totin' 'em."

Floyd nodded thanks to both Fannie and Abe while offering a feeble smile. Tabor could see in his eyes, though, that Floyd had sunken once again into feeling unworthy of the task at hand. A fact, that Tabor found worrisome in the least.

Soon the little party broke apart as all moved to prepare for a few hours of sleep. Tabor found his way to Floyd's side and stood silently studying the short bull of a man as he rolled out his bedding.

"You got something to say?" Floyd mumbled.

"No. But fear you do," Tabor said softly.

Floyd stood erect and stretched his back while emitting a low moan. "Sure wish those two were here with us now."

"That is a wish that can never come true."

"I can wish it all the same."

"No arguing with that," Tabor said before standing quietly, waiting for Floyd to go ahead and speak his mind.

"By this time tomorrow, we might have done met up with the Apache and Laughing Billy," Floyd said as if just thinking out loud.

"Strong possibility of such," Tabor agreed.

Now, Floyd studied Tabor and finally asked, "Are you afraid?"

"You know the answer to that question. The one begging to be answered though is…are you afraid?"

"Never went into a fight that I didn't feel some fear."

Tabor offered a smile, "But it never stopped you in the past, and it will not stop you tomorrow."

Floyd moved his head to look in the direction of the other men preparing for the night. "If tomorrow is the day…some of them most definitely won't be left standing."

"I would agree most definitely."

Floyd turned his head to the heavens as if counting the stars above their heads. Moments later he lowered his gaze to stare Tabor in the eyes. "Will you stand with me tomorrow?"

"Right now," Tabor sighed, "I certainly intend to do so."

His answer didn't seem to bring Floyd peace of mind. At the moment though, it was the best Tabor could offer.

* * * *

The Apache had enough of the insane laughter for one day.

"Time to get some sleep. We enter Beaver City tomorrow," he said, as he threw enough logs on the fire to keep it ablaze through the night.

Laughing Billy whooped with laughter over the fact. "How many townsfolk you think we must kill, JP?"

"We will kill those in need of killing."

"Yeah, but how many? Ten? Twenty?" Bemo guffawed.

"I hope to kill none."

"None?" Bemo sputtered.

As he did often, the Apache turned to study the grinning face. "Why do you find joy in killing?"

"Oh, now, do not start with those hard to answer question of yours," Bemo giggled. "Besides, you gonna tell me you do not enjoy killing?"

"Killing is what I do. It does not bother me, but I find no satisfaction in it either."

Bemo seemed to find that knee slapping funny.

"Why do you laugh so much?"

"Told you before, ain't none of your business, Injun."

"Soon enough, one of us will die. Death will not touch me, so it must be you. Before you die, I would like to know why you laugh."

Bemo, as he so often did, laughed without merriment. Now he looked away and snickered, "I was told that I was laughing when they found me."

"When found by whom?"

"Soldiers. I was six-years-old. They also tell me, that I had a mama, and papa, and two older sisters. Comanche killed them all.

Raped my mama and sisters. No matter to me," Bemo laughed, "'cause I don't remember them ever being."

"You laughed before the Comanche fell upon you," the Apache said.

"And how the hell would you know that?" Bemo snickered.

"That is why you were spared. They thought you possessed by evil spirits."

"You mean like a demon?"

"Yes."

"They feared me?" Bemo giggled.

"Possibly."

"Then you must also fear me, Injun."

The Apache awarded his cohort with a rare smile. "I am most comfortable in the company of demons, White Man."

* * * *

Eden Ledford quietly closed the door behind him and moved on tip toes through the small house to put away his weaponry. He worked to remove his clothing when Rose's voice called from the bedroom.

"The hour is late."

"Just finished making my rounds, Rose."

Stripped to his under garments, Eden slipped into the bed next to his young wife.

"You said you would only do this for a year," Rose whispered.

"Has that much time passed?" Eden asked.

"That and nearly a month more."

Eden sighed long and hard as he settled beneath the covers. Rose had not wanted him to take the job from the very start and reminded him of it daily.

"What else can I do?" he asked.

"You sought to open a dry goods store."

"And we are putting money aside to do just that," Eden said softly.

After gaining his release from the army, Eden brought his new bride back to his hometown. Oh, how things changed in his absence. The Lone Star and Red Bull Saloons were closed and now the two empty buildings stood boarded up. Even harder for Eden to believe, both the Four Deuces and The Tackett Ranches were no more. Good ol' Ben Tackett died in terrible fashion, and the despicable rascal Stew Graybow fled out of fear for his life. Since the ranches met their demise and the two bars subsequently went out of business, Eden's hometown of Beaver City grew downright peaceful.

While in the army, young Lieutenant Ledford participated in forcing the last of the renegade Comanche to surrender and move peaceably to reservations. Eden returned home with only one marketable skill: a proficient handling of firearms. The mayor, Dick Thurman, wasted no time in offering Eden the job of town marshal, and Eden, against Rose's wishes, accepted the position. Ever since, he did his damnedest to convince her that because of the actions of his predecessor, CB Wooly, Beaver City posed no significant threat to a man carrying a badge. As to date, nothing happened to prove him wrong.

"Rose," he said tenderly, "I need one more year of doing this job. By then, we will have the money to open our store."

His wife sighed long and hard before shaking her head and saying, "You can only do it for seven, or eight months at the most."

Puzzled, Eden asked, "What difference would four or five months make?"

Rose snuggled in beside Eden before responding, "My monthly sickness has abandoned me twice in a roll."

Eden shot upright in bed. "You're carrying my baby?"

"I do suspect so."

The marshal of Beaver City felt overcome with a numbness of sorts – a mixture of natural joy, and a sudden foreboding that sprouted without explanation.

* * * *

Graybow laid on his back staring up at the stars. He'd spent much of his life doing so, but in his later years, grew accustomed to the pleasures of a comfortable bed beneath the ceiling of a fine house. Within a few days, at the longest, he would be back in the grand house he'd toiled to build with his own hands.

Not out of choice, but by luck of the draw, if one considered such as luck, Graybow never experienced sharing his home with a special woman. Only days now stood in the way of that being a reality. Martha Henry, bedded down beside her coach not thirty feet in the distance, had not displayed any of the feelings toward Graybow that he uncontrollably felt for her, but he harbored no discouragement. She had yet to see the house awaiting her arrival.

Once home, Graybow would confront the fact that warrants for his arrest no doubt existed. For now, he simply pitied any poor son of a bitch brave enough, or stupid enough, to attempt serving such warrants.

* * * *

"You tend to win a lot more times than you lose, Kid."

Jack Friday paused from gathering the last of his winnings to stare across the dwindling campfire at the man that they all knew only as, "Bear." The five did not know if it was his given name, family name, or just a nickname describing his physical characteristics and disposition. He'd never offered clarification, and the others in the group didn't truly give a damn one way or the other.

"Are you complementing my luck, Bear," Friday said in a low voice, "or do you accuse me of cheating?"

Bear leaned forward and pointed an index finger at Friday's face. "Do not waggle a tongue at me, Kid, or I will jerk it out of your mouth and stuff it up your ass."

Pink Corning gathered the cards to put them away for the night, but now placed a hand on Friday's shoulder to keep him in place.

"Ain't no sense in ending the night in ugliness," Pink said to Bear.

"Oh, I would disagree," Tim Swonger grinned. "I would enjoy seeing a good fight."

"Would not be a fight to it," Bear hissed at Swonger.

"You're right, Bear," Friday nodded. "I wouldn't fight you. I would simply gut you like Sunday's chicken."

Bear jumped to his feet, and Bodie Bowman, the closest one to Bear's size, stood and moved to stand between Friday and Bear. "The old man warned there would be no fightin' amongst us. I intend to draw every cent he has promised."

"I stand with Bowman," Pink said, "No need in us fighting each other. We will have fighting to do a' plenty soon enough."

Friday shrugged Pink's hand off his shoulder. The interference from the others did not necessary delight him, but then again, a fight with the huge man could go south awfully fast. All again took their seats. A quick glimpse around the campfire, and into the faces of the others, suggested to Friday that they all now dwelt on the possibilities of tangling with the men Graybow listed as possible adversaries.

First there was the law. From what Friday gathered, the men in this circle could take on any number of men wearing badges and held no qualms in doing so. The deputy, Floyd Danner, held the reputation of one hell of a scrapper, but not all that formidable with a gun. Graybow had said that Danner might be accompanied by a skilled marksman named Walt Tabor, who, according to Graybow, proved no more than a sniveling coward when shooting at anything that could shoot back. That left the Indian, and his co-hart, the crazy man that laughed. Graybow expressed a feeling that one or both might have returned to his house, claiming it as their own, and would not look kindly upon eviction. These two could pose a deadly threat, but when it came right down to it, Friday liked the odds of Graybow's five against only two, no matter how deadly those two had proven in the past.

CHAPTER NINE

Turned to Pandemonium

Danner's heart felt heavier than a circus fat lady. None had been too talkative while tearing down camp a few hours past. Now, he assumed that they all made their way down the road dreading how this day might end. Of course, there was the matter of possibly confronting the Apache and Laughing Billy Bemo. That outcome, he left to speculation, and the responsibility he felt to his men, accounted for only about half of the weight pressing heavily on his innards.

What was not left to speculation was the parting with the Francis twins. It stood pitifully imminent. Sometime in mere hours to come, there would be a splitting of ways with the lovely young women. No doubt about it.

Danner fought at the dread as Walt pulled up alongside him.

"You have little to say today," Walt said.

"And thank the Good Lord," Danner sighed, "so do you."

Walt nodded his head and rode alongside Danner a few more minutes before opening his mouth yet again. "Are you preparing your goodbyes?"

"Wishing it did not have to be," Danner grumbled.

"Oh, well, it does not *have* to be."

Danner turned a scowl upon Walt. "Yes, it *has* to be."

"Are you going to tell me, Floyd, that you have not considered the possibility of just following these young ladies right on into their new lives?"

"I guess you have, Walt?"

"Does not matter what I've considered. I'm not in charge."

"You can do what you want," Danner growled.

"What I *want*, Floyd Danner, is to follow you right into hell if need be."

"You have that much desire to win back my respect, Walt?"

Tabor turned a weary smile on Danner. "I have that much desire to win back the respect of my own self."

"Well, hell could be waiting at the end of this day. You most likely will get that chance."

"I'll allow you to ride on by yourself now, Floyd. I have to prepare my own goodbyes."

"Good luck with that, Walt," Danner said before spurring his horse to pull away from a man that tended to make him think deeper than maybe he proved capable.

* * * *

Every town had its own sound that it made when everything went day to day normal. At a late afternoon hour, that sound now penetrated the thin walls of the Smith Dry Goods Store, emphasizing the peace Margaret Smith now practically took for granted in her humdrum life. Her days of keeping books, stocking shelves, and doing her best to be a good wife to Elijah Smith held none of the dangers of the horrible past. Enough time had now dwindled that she did not dwell constantly on the fact of being one of the very last to see CB

Wooly still alive. The "what might have beens," of that dear man living on, no longer tormented her sleep. She no longer felt guilt for the fact that she would have left pitiful Elijah, had CB only found the lack of integrity to ask her to do so. All of that now lay dead in a grave far, far away in a place named Stillwater, located somewhere in the Oklahoma Territory. The community she'd once referred to as "*Blood City,*" now thrived in relative peace because of the body rotting in that grave.

The slow clomping of hooves on the hard-packed dirt street, the relaxed pace of heels connecting with the board walk, distant chatter, the occasional sound of a child's laughter, or a mother's muted reprimand of unruly children, all mixed and mingled and wafted through the store's walls to assure Margaret that beyond her door, all was normal and regular in the town of Beaver City.

Margaret positioned a step-stool to reach a top shelf when Elijah came in from the storage room wearing his bowler and pulling on his coat. "Off to the city council meeting. Can I get you anything while I am out and about?"

"I don't know what it would be," Margret said, fighting off the urge to add, *I already have all a woman could possibly want in No Man's Land.* However, she spared him from her sarcasm, as she tried so hard to do these days.

In her husband's absence, Margaret busied herself with tasks she could do in her sleep. She had no idea how much time passed when suddenly the day to day normal sounds of her town went awry.

Hooves thundered. Heels on planks broke into a run. Men bellowed. Mothers screamed for children to draw near. Margaret moved toward the door when it shot open and Elijah burst through in an all-out pant, slamming the door behind him and leaning back against it as to block the entrance to intruders.

"Elijah! What in the world?"

"Up the street!" he gasped. "Just sitting their horses. Side by side."

"Who, Elijah?"

He just shook his head as if in utter disbelief while fighting to catch his breath. Margaret grabbed him by his shoulders and moved him aside.

"No!" he thundered. "Do not go out there for goodness sake!"

Margaret hadn't built this marriage on obeying her man. She threw the door open and stepped out on the planked sidewalk. Her eyes were drawn to the site of people fleeing to her left. She turned her head to the right and gasped at the site.

There was no mistaking the Apache and Laughing Billy Bemo. As Elijah said, they simply sat...and watched as the town before them began to crumble.

* * * *

"We should have rode in with guns blazing," Bemo snickered his objection.

The Apache surveyed the chaos to their front and shook his head. "No need. Our appearance alone is clearing the streets."

"Mighty fine being recognized," Bemo giggled.

"It is not always a good thing, but this time it serves our need."

When the main street stood empty, the Apache spoke Latin to the black stallion, and it pranced forward at a fast walk.

"Guess it is time to go, horse," Bemo chuckled to his mount, "Even though nobody had the common courtesy to tell you and me."

The Apache ignored the remark. He pulled the stallion to a halt in front of the telegraph office and dismounted in the fashion of his people by throwing his right leg up and over the horse's neck, and springing to the ground. "You stay here and watch the street," he said to Bemo.

"Yes, sir, boss man," Bemo laughed tauntingly.

The Apache walked into the office with his hands on his guns but did not pull them from their holsters. A tall man resembling a skinny and crooked pole cringed in a corner.

"Have you sent messages of our arrival?" the Apache asked calmly.

"No, sir. Sure did not. No, sir," the man whimpered.

"Why not?"

"I do only as instructed, sir. No one instructed me to do so."

"You know who I am?"

"Oh, yes sir. I know, sir…do spare my life!"

"This time," the Apache whispered, "I came only to destroy your means of communication."

With that, he pulled both pistols and put three bullets from each into the man's telegraphing device.

After holstering his weapons, he walked to within touching distance of the quivering man. "Make repairs, and the next time you see me, I will be here to destroy you."

* * * *

Town Marshal Eden Ledford sat up in bed from his afternoon nap and shook his head to shake away the sleep.

Gunfire?

"Rose!" he bellowed as he swung his feet from the bed, sitting upright to pull his suspenders up and over his shoulders.

Rose rushed into the bedroom and threw herself at Eden. "Do not go!" she screamed.

Eden gently moved her aside and stood from his bed. "I heard gunfire."

"Yes, yes," she moaned with tears starting to fill her eyes. "The town has turned to pandemonium!"

"What? Why?" Eden grasped for answers.

"Do not know! Only moments ago, a terrible ruckus stirred the streets."

Eden moved to retrieve his sidearm and rifle. Rose fled to the front of the house and pressed herself against the door. "You will not go out there."

Then a panicked pounding fell upon the other side of the door. With a Smith and Wesson at the ready, Eden hurried to a side window, carefully pulled back the curtain, and saw Dick Thurman on his stoop.

"Move aside, Rose," he said gently, "it's only Mayor Thurman."

Eden opened the door, and Thurman rushed in. "The Apache and Laughing Billy Bemo!" he blurted.

"Why are they here?" Eden said as a malignant lump seemed to sprout deep in his guts.

"Do not know," the mayor exclaimed, "but I do know, you cannot face them alone. It would be suicidal."

"What am I to do?" Eden asked.

"What we will all be doing," Thurman sighed, "Waiting and watching and praying to God."

* * * *

"Me, Zed, and Abe will ride on up ahead at a slow pace, Floyd," Hound Olivo said, looking down from his horse at the dismounted Danner.

"Whatever you think proper, Hound," Danner nodded absently, his mind on a graver matter.

Danner stood in the crossroads where the path they'd traveled continued west, and an unfamiliar one snaked to the north. Fannie and Annie were crawling down from their wagon, and Walt Tabor, still mounted, lingered at a distance.

In their still shy manner, Hound, Zed, and Abe removed their hats, and wished the ladies an awkward farewell. Once they moved on, Danner pulled in a deep breath of air and walked in Fannie's direction. Annie was already moving toward Tabor. It felt much easier watching those two as Danner took one painful step after another. Tabor dismounted as Annie grew nearer but remained beside his horse.

"Am I that painful to look at, Floyd Danner?" Fannie called out to him.

He waited until face to face before sighing, "In this situation, you are, indeed, most painful to look upon, but not for reasons of your physical appearance."

"I do so love your way with words, dear sir," Fannie smiled, but not with glee.

"Goodbyes do not come easy for me," Danner said, when nothing else seemed appropriate.

"This one will not be easy for me either," Fannie agreed.

Danner scuffed the ground with the toe of his boot before finding the courage to ask, "May I, just for a moment, embrace you in my arms?"

"I would be disappointed if you did not."

Danner took Fannie in his arms, and it felt heavenly and still hurt like hell. He wanted to hold her forever and sensed she would be fine with him doing so. Sadly, he did not, at the moment, have forever.

They pulled apart and for moments stared deeply into each other's eyes.

"When my business is concluded, and if I stand able, may I come to find you?" He asked.

"Again, I would be disappointed if you did not."

He took her by the hand and they walked to his horse. Without looking in her eyes again, he swung into the saddle.

"May God go with you, Floyd Danner," she said with a quiver in her voice.

Danner did not know if God traveled with any man set on killing other men but did not say as much. Instead, he doffed his hat, winked, did his best to smile, and started his horse away at a walk. He did not look back, but soon heard Walt coming up behind him. After Walt pulled aside him, the two men rode for minutes without speaking.

Finally, without looking at the man beside him, Danner asked, "Did you promise to see her again?"

"I don't make promises I may not be able to keep."

Danner turned a doubtful eye on Walt.

"What I mean is," Tabor said without meeting his gaze, "that I no longer make promises I may not be able to keep."

As if both men knew the mind of the other, they spurred their horses at the exact moment and tore off in a gallop to catch up with their friends.

* * * *

Eden Ledford refused to stay cooped up in the small house a moment longer with his frantic wife. Making adamant promises to go no further, he readied his guns and started for the jail. It did his mind and heart no good having to tear away from Rose's frantic attempts to keep him within her grasp.

He walked the streets with his Winchester at port arms and marveled on the emptiness of the streets at such an early hour. Beaver City seemed a ghost town. In the jail, he worked at cleaning a double-barreled shotgun when the door banged open and Rowland Beans burst inside. Eden whirled and leveled the shotgun at Beans, feeling immediately inept and stupid. The shotgun bore no shells. How could a man so unnerved face the likes of the Apache and Bemo when forced to do so?

"They want you, Marshal," Beans, out of breath, huffed. "They sent me to fetch you."

Eden at least had enough senses about him not to ask who "they" were.

"So, they settled at your place, Rowland?"

Beans now owned the only bar in town and kept three rooms above to let to travelers. "Emptied the place out, Marshal. Ran two guests from the upstairs rooms. Said my place would be their headquarters."

"Headquarters?" Eden questioned. When Beans offered no response but a shrug of his shoulders, and an unknowing shake of his head, Eden considered the motivations and implications, and came to no conclusion that offered comfort.

Eden took a deep breath and inserted two shells into the shotgun.

"The Indian, Marshal, said he had no intent to kill you...unless you was of a mind to die."

"I'm not of a mind to die, Rowland. You don't believe I am walking into an ambush?"

"I can't promise a thing, Marshal, but the crazy one, the one that laughs, said he would look me up and shoot me until I was dead, if I didn't come back with you at my side."

"Would not want that to happen, Rowland," Eden said as he slowly came to his feet. After a few seconds of deep breathing to clear his mind, and strengthen his legs, he started toward the door.

"Rowland, instead of at my side, I insist you stay a good safe distance to my back."

Rowland Beans did not object.

* * * *

The Marshal walked a slow but steady pace from his jail in the direction of the Beaver City Saloon. Thoughts bounced in his mind of his wife, the badge he wore, and the battles he'd fought, along with the men he'd watched die. With the exception of only a few, none proved the act to be an easy one. Some cried. Some screamed. Most withered in great agony while taking their final breaths. Too many went out doing it all at the same time. In Eden's experience, even the least likely, often gave up their dignity with their soul. Even Sergeant Shane Steltler proved no exception.

Steltler, a career soldier, enlisted at the age of seventeen, from that point to the time of his death, he'd spent all but four of his adult years in the United States Army. The four years he did not serve the Union, he fought for the south in the War Against the States. Steltler followed ol' General Lee through the most horrific battles of the war. By the time he was allowed once again to wear blue, no man could claim to be more battle hardened. Eden never met a man more capable of dealing relentless death to the enemy. He never knew a man who seemed less fearful of meeting his maker. Sergeant Steltler so many times looked death in the face only to wink and grin.

Eden stood beside the old soldier the day the Sergeant caught his appointed arrows. One to the right thigh. One to the small of the back. One clean through his neck. While Eden returned fire at charging Comanches, Steltler spun in place alternating at grabbing and tugging on the three bloody arrows, while all along, looking skyward and screaming at the heavens.

"No, Dear God! Do not forsake me now!"

Foamy blood poured from his mouth and matted in the thick gray facial hair surrounding his face.

"Noooooooo," he wailed, "Send me not to hell, Dear God above!"

Soon enough he crumbled to his knees, still tugging on one arrow and then another, and his eyes started to glaze.

"Mama? Is that you? I cannot reach your lovin' hand, for the demons are dragging me to hell!"

Sergeant Shane Steltler toppled face first, and in the dirt, his legs kicked in a manner that seemed he only lived at that awful moment from the waist down. When finally, he breathed his last, Eden heard the great expelling of gas, and the smell of shit suddenly permeated the air. The toughest man Eden ever met, did not bravely fight death as he'd fought in life, and went out shitting his trousers.

Eden stopped in mid stride and considered the fact he did not have to take one step further. He could flee to his house, grab his wife and a few possessions, and leave Beaver City forever. The only downfall would be that Rowland Beans would die as a result of Eden's decision. Then, Rose and their unborn child would be forced to live life with a man that hated himself. No good could come from such, and so he walked on.

* * * *

The Apache leaned with his back against the bar and his arms crossed over his chest when a voice called from out in the street.

"This is Marshal Eden Ledford. What business do you have with me?"

The Apache did not move from his relaxed position but paused before responding to look across the room at Laughing Billy sitting on the steps leading to the upstairs. He held a pistol in each hand and giggled as if naked women pranced before him.

The Apache turned his head back toward the door. "Is the barkeep Beans with you, Marshal?"

"He is," the voice responded.

"Send him in first," the Apache ordered.

"Do you mean to do him harm?" the Marshal called.

"Do you care if I do him harm?"

"I most certainly do," Ledford responded.

"If you do as told, I will spare him from a terrible death."

The Apache heard an exchange of words outside the door that he could not make-out. A moment later, Rowland Beans slowly entered the bar like a dog kicked once too many times. The Apache motioned his head to send the man behind the bar where he belonged. Bemo laughed as if tickled by unseen hands.

"Will you do as I have asked?" the Apache asked Bemo.

"As long as it continues to suit me I will," Bemo hee-hawed.

The Apache did not like the response, but only expressed such with a sharp glance at the laughing idiot.

"Marshal," he called out. "You may enter now. I strongly suggest you do so with your hands empty."

The door opened and a young man, tall and slim, walked in standing erect. His eyes first fell upon the Apache, but quickly scanned the room to find Bemo perched on the stairs with two pistols pointed in his direction. The coat the marshal wore did not conceal the handgun stuck down the front of his trousers. But his arms remained at his sides. The young lawman looked alert and on edge, but did not appear overly fearful. The Apache held his demeanor in respect.

"Mr. Beans tells me you were a cavalry man. I am Apache. Did you hunt and kill my people?"

The marshal took in a deep breath and raised his chin in defiance. "I never patrolled the regions west of Texas," he said evenly.

"You killed the Comanche?"

"When my duty required it," Ledford nodded, "I did so."

The Apache nodded his head in return. "I have no qualms with that. They are a filthy and despicable people by nature."

Bemo, giggling all along now cackled like a madman. Ledford half turned his head to stare with disgust at Bemo.

"Do not turn the evil eye on me, law-dog," Bemo thundered with laughter, "or I will surely shoot you betwixt the eyeballs!"

Before turning his head back to face the Apache, Ledford exhaled as if ridding his nostrils from the stench of excrement. "What do you want with me?"

"I have a job for you to do."

"I do not work for you," the marshal said through gritted teeth.

The Apache dropped his hands to rest on his holstered pistols and calmly pushed away from the bar. He took steps that put him only feet in front of Ledford. The young man stiffened but stood his ground.

"Mr. Beans tells us that you have a pretty young wife. Do you wish that she remain as such?"

The marshal took an aggressive step forward and all but shouted, "You do not…"

The Apache pulled both pistols and leveled them at the marshal's face.

"You do not," he said calmly, "take that tone with me. Take a good look at the man on the stairs. They call him Laughing Billy Bemo, but his laughter does not depict his evil soul. I will shoot you now, and he will then have his way with your young wife. The results will be most horrific."

Ledford was now trembling, but not from fear. Rage contorted his face, but he did turn his head to silently consider the man now bellowing laughter.

"Shoot him, Injun! Shoot the law-dog! Let me at that woman!"

Suddenly, Ledford's shoulders slumped and he dropped his eyes to stare at the planked floor. "What do you require of me?" he mumbled.

"I only ask that you post yourself on the hills south of town. When riders come, and they will come, I require that you provide me advance warning."

The marshal's eyes remained on the floor at his feet as he considered the assignment. "In doing so, I will forsake the people of this town. I will be considered both a traitor and a coward."

"Most likely," the Apache nodded, "but the lives of both you and your woman will be spared."

Ledford raised his eyes to stare into the face of the Apache, "My life be damned. I only care for the safety of my wife. Do I have your word that no harm will come to her?"

The Apache turned to glare at Bemo. "You do as asked, and I will die before any harm comes to her."

After a defeated nod of his head, Ledford turned and started for the door.

"So as to guarantee your peace of mind, Marshal," the Apache said to his back, "Be it known, I am not capable of dying."

The marshal of Beaver City stopped and turned slowly in place, but his eyes did not fall on the Apache. His final words were spoken to the man behind the bar.

"Rowland Beans, you talk too damned much."

CHAPTER TEN

Not Again

Zed Martin pulled on his reigns and motioned Danner forward. "The cabin is around this bend. No more than a quarter of a mile, Floyd."

Danner looked up at the full moon and cursed it for being in place.

"Damn, Zed," he mumbled, "trees are few and far apart in this region."

"And like I told you before, Floyd, ain't not a one around that shack."

"Full moon and no trees," Danner grumbled. "We might as well be carrying torches and singing Dixie at the top of our lungs."

"It's awfully late, Floyd. Maybe they be sleepin'," Zed responded.

"Maybe," Danner nodded, "but not likely." He signaled for the others to gather in close.

"We'll tie the horses here and travel the remaining distance on foot. When we get closer and get the lay of the land, we'll make our final plans."

As the men dismounted and tied their horses to what semblance of trees existed, Abe moved up close to Danner.

"Floyd, I's be darker than this night. Not likely to be spotted as you whities, and I means no dis'spect…"

"No disrespect taken. Go on, Abe," Danner said, unable even in this situation not to grin.

"Why's I done my's share of scoutin'. I can move ahead of you's boys and return in the blinks of a cat's eye if'n I sees any thang not right."

Danner patted Abe on the back, grinning again, and said, "Why, that is a splendid idea, Abe. Should have thought of it myself."

"You gots tons on you's mind rights now, Floyd. A tad bit of thinkin' is the leasts I's can do."

"And fine thinking it was, Abe. You go ahead, and we'll remain in place a while before following behind you.

In the bright glow of the moon, Danner could clearly see the wide smile on Abe's face. As his scout tore off in a near run, Danner said a silent prayer for Abe and the rest as well.

* * * *

Danner felt as exposed as a bride on her wedding night. However, no choice existed but to move forward. His men remained silent and took advantage of what little cover and concealment existed. Danner knew they'd covered a fair piece of the quarter mile and was about to confer with Zed when suddenly he observed Abe's form moving at a fast pace back to his position.

Danner and the others squatted in place and Abe soon dropped to a knee next to him.

"Floyd, they's cryin' up ahead."

"Crying?"

"Yes, sir, just a terrible wailin'. I's just close enough to sees that cabin at a fur distance whens I hears a mournful moanin' likes a woman passin' a chil'."

"A woman?"

"Yes, sir, believes so."

Zed moved closer. "Must be that awful widow woman, Floyd."

"Must be," Danner nodded. "But I wonder why she would be wailing?"

Walt offered a response, "The Apache and Laughing Billy Bemo seems reason enough for me."

Danner hoped with all his might that the moonlight allowed Walt to see the look Danner gave him.

"Well," Danner started with nods of his head, "Guess we'll find out soon enough what plagues the woman. Let's get on to the business at hand."

Sooner than Danner wanted it to be, the cabin appeared in the distance. No lights shined from within, and nothing moved on the outside. Within a few more yards of travel, Danner, in fact, heard the crying of a female voice. He waived for Walt to move up beside him.

"You and I'll go ahead from here. Get close enough to determine what we do next."

He felt a sense of relief when Walt simply responded, "Okay."

He and Walt spread the word for the others to remain in place, once done, they moved out slowly at a crouch with rifles at the ready. Danner first spotted the outhouse positioned a good forty yards from the cabin. He used a hand on Walt's elbow to steer him in that direction. When they reached the rickety structure, they crowded each other to hide behind the narrow back wall.

"You peek to one side, and I will peek to the other," he whispered to Walt.

Both men peeked, and then fell back in place.

"Damn!" Walt exclaimed in a whisper.

"You see something?"

"Sure did, but don't exactly know what I did see. Let me peek again."

Walt lingered in his peek longer this time and had an answer as he sprung back in place.

"I see the woman, Floyd. Looks to be kneeling on the ground this side of the corral. Something is on the ground beside her, but I can't make it out."

Danner shook his head to clear it and felt relieved when an option popped to mind. "Sun up cannot be far in the distance. I suggest we take up positions around the cabin and wait to see what stirs at dawn's breaking."

Walt laid a hand on his shoulder. "I do declare, Floyd, I find that to be a splendid suggestion."

Out of sheer stubbornness, Danner fought off the desire to feel complimented by Walt's approval.

* * * *

Sawbuck Sam had tracked and scouted men in this type of terrain plenty times before, but his duty then did not require that he draw near enough to hear their conversations. With so few things to conceal his damned movement, he knew for sure if the men he trailed were Comanche, Sawbuck would by now be roasting on a damned pit. These men, thank the Good Lord, were downright pitiful when it came to an awareness of their surroundings. Damned, if they didn't act like hounds after a coon. When a hound pursues a coon, Sawbuck knew for sure, hounds don't see nothing but the damned coon.

As the sun poked at the horizon, Sawbuck watched the cabin and the dispersed men from an ancient spy glass. He feared this cabin might hold the Indian and the laughing bastard. Under his breath, Sawbuck cursed the open prairie land from which he'd tracked Danner and his damned men for the past couple of days. In that time, he'd not been able to get close enough to hear their discussions. If they found the damned men they sought here, Sawbuck's plan would be, in fact, damned. Without him first meeting up with those outlaws, he feared Floyd Danner would kill him for sure.

* * * *

Now certain of what he looked upon in the first lighting of the eastern sky, Hound Olivo all but crawled on hands and knees to reach Danner. As luck would have it, he'd been placed nearest to the figure Walt thought he'd seen mere hours ago.

"It's for sure a woman," he announced to Floyd. "And looks to be yet another woman lying on the ground right behind her."

Olivo waited for directions as he watched Floyd chew on the news he just delivered.

"I can't understand why two women would be left outside," Danner said as he stared in the direction from which Olivo had scurried. "Yet, they are, and that does not change what we now have to do. Hurry back to your position, Hound. When I think you are there, I'll fire my shots."

Olivo stooped at his assigned spot for one hellaciously long minute before two rifle shots broke the silence of a dawning new day. Olivo trained his rifle on the cabin, while hoping and praying this would not be the last new day he drew breath to witness.

From the distance separating them, Olivo heard Floyd's hollered demand.

"We have you surrounded! Come out of that cabin, or we'll fill it with flying lead!"

Olivo had known what to expect since the simple plan was made. The one thing he had not expected, which was nothing at all, now played out to his front. No comments were returned. Nothing moved. Nothing changed. Olivo waited for Floyd's next command, which would not be leveled at the shoddy cabin. It came not soon enough for Olivo but did in fact come.

"Open fire, boys!" Floyd shouted.

Olivo, along with the others, did as told earlier and emptied a full complement of rounds from his Winchester into the walls of the small structure. When the smoke cleared, Olivo observed that still nothing moved. Nothing changed. He quickly reloaded the rifle and waited for what, he did not know.

"Hold your positions, fellers, and cover me," Floyd bellowed. "I'm going in there."

Olivo jerked his head in Floyd's direction and observed him stand and start for the cabin. He watched as Floyd slowly advanced on the cabin, and then gawked at the site of Abe running up to Floyd's side.

* * * *

Danner did not take his eyes off the cabin and held his rifle pointed at the front door. "Get back to your position, Abe," he ordered.

"Ain't gonna, Floyd... unless you's intend to boss me likes a slave."

"This is my job, Abe."

"No, sir, you's too impo'tent to goes walkin' through that door. That be a job fo' me and this here scatter-gun."

Danner could not argue that Abe's shotgun would be most effective in the confinements of the shack, still, he balked at sending one of his men into a situation that could end up killing him. Knowing precious minutes were slipping away, he reluctantly gave into the logic.

"Go then. I'll cover you from here."

Again, there appeared a wide and toothy smile before Abe bolted toward the cabin at a full out run. Danner watched as the big man ran right through the closed door, sending it flying apart in splinters. From his position he heard Abe's powerful weapon fire once, twice, and a third time. Then Danner, too, sprang into a run and noticed all the others doing the same. He made it to within a couple of yards of the destroyed opening when Abe stepped out with the shotgun resting on a shoulder.

"Ain't be a damned nobody in the place," Abe grinned. "Had they been, I's ripped thems apart with this here shotgun."

Danner took several deep breaths of cleansing air before his mind turned to the women nearby. Walt was already beside them on bent knee, and Danner could see his lips moving to form words.

"They alive, Walt?" He called out as he started toward them.

"One is for sure, but I can't tell about the other. Looks as if they were bound together at one point, but the ropes have loosened."

Danner reached the downed women and Walt at about the same time as all the others.

Zed pointed to the one still sitting partially upright, "That one is the widow woman. Never seen the other."

Floyd, along with the others, murmured comments and curses on the women's horribly abused condition. Both had been gagged. The woman on the ground still had hers in place. The widow woman's had slipped down on her neck.

"Floyd," Walt spoke above the others, "These women need help, and they best get it quickly."

"I can tell that by looking at them, Walt, but I ain't no doctor, and have no idea where a doctor can be found, and…"

"Annie Francis has done some nursing, Floyd," Walt interrupted Danner's rant, "and she told me Fannie lent her a hand from time to time."

Danner suddenly wanted to both hit and hug Walt, but instead he jerked his head toward Hound. "You mind taking that big powerful horse of yours to try to find those ladies and bring them back here, Hound? I would send you with help, but if that Indian and Bemo show up here, I fear we will need every hand we can get."

It did not surprise Danner that Hound simply took off at a quick pace in the direction they'd left their horses. The man seemed to hoard his words as much as some men did their money.

Danner turned his attention to Zed and Abe, "If you two will set up a watch, Walt and I will move these two into the cabin and do what we can to make them comfortable."

Zed took out with Abe at his side, but called over his shoulder, "If'n you want them to be comfortable, best not take them in that pitiful shack. The stench alone will finish them off for sure."

* * * *

Elijah Smith stared at his face in the oval mirror. Down below the living quarters, he knew his wife busied herself in the store to take her mind off what he could not.

When bad men in the past held their town hostage, he'd done nothing, and Margaret Smith despised him for it. Had CB Wooly bested The Apache and Laughing Billy Bemo, Smith didn't doubt that he would have lost his wife to a man who hadn't feared taking action. On that terrible day, after the smoke cleared from the shots Stew Graybow fired to finish off Wooly, Smith had been the first to venture into the street. It fell to him to drag his torn and bloody remains to the undertaker. As Smith tugged, he looked down into open eyes that seemed to stare back, penetrating Smith's very soul. Then and there, he swore on the blood that trailed his sorrowful path that he would never again hide behind another man's gun, badge, or reputation.

Staring into the mirror, he tried so hard to look beyond his disappointing features to see instead the face of CB Wooly, but even now his life-long nemesis, called a weakness of spine, blocked his ability to do so. Even such a vivid memory of that blood-stained face could not trump fear. Both unconsciously and uncontrollably, Smith's head started to move slowly back and forth as he stared deeply into his own eyes, and began to declare,

"Not again…Not again…Not again…"

* * * *

Margaret thought it ironic that whom they considered their one and only hope, now sat posted on the outskirts of town waiting to alert the Apache and Bemo of an unknown force, that if could come unannounced, might rid Beaver City of its latest form of plague. Margaret did not blame the town marshal. He truly had no choice.

Mayor Dick Thurman had ridden out to where a rejected Eden Ledford sat on his horse staring at the horizon, and Thurman brought back the news of Ledford's dilemma. That news spread through the community like wild fire, leaving all who heard it void of any hope of preventing two very bad men from doing whatever they pleased to a helpless town.

Margaret knew she differed from the rest, because her overwhelming emotion was not that of fear or dread, but instead, indifference. The realization had crept upon her like a dense fog, bringing both relief and sorrow. Sometime over the past few hours, she'd surrendered to the fact that the last thing she truly cared about, now lay being devoured by worms deep in a grave.

Just a few hours earlier, had she heard the exterior door upstairs being opened, as she did now, she would have tried so hard to truly care where it might be that her husband was headed. Now though, hearing his brogans making their descent on the outside stairs, Margaret simply did not give a damn.

* * * *

Zed's memories of the awful cabin proved to be most accurate. Danner could not have placed an ailing pig in there to die, even if he didn't like the pig. He'd worked with Walt to position their own bedrolls in order to make the women as comfortable as possible on the ground. Walt patiently tried to force drops of water down the dark-haired woman's throat. This one had yet to show any signs of life other than faint and sporadic breathing. Danner experienced better luck with the one whose awful tangle of hair might have been golden, if ever subjected to a good washing. She now was mumbling, taking greater sips of water, and even chewing, ever so slowly, on bits of a biscuit Danner pinched off in crumbs. At midday, the blonde opened her eyes and squinted at the glaring sun overhead.

"Can you tell me your name?" Danner asked, enthused by her sudden awareness.

After long seconds of trying to clear her throat, the woman finally managed to faintly reply, "Does not matter."

"Are you still Bemo's woman?"

She turned wild-looking eyes on him, and for long moments did nothing but stare with what looked like anger or hatred or both.

With great effort, she finally asked, "Have you come to kill him?"

"I have come to insure justice is done…one way or another."

The woman closed her eyes and took deep breathes of air before feebly raising a hand and motioning Danner to draw near. His ear all but touched her lips before words were issued. Once they were, Danner shot upright.

"What did she say?" Walt asked.

Ignoring Walt, Danner asked the woman, "Are you sure of this?"

Again, efforts to clear her throat were made that resulted in her voice squeaking out, "The Indian said so."

Danner shot to his feet and called out loud for Zed and Abe to hear, "Come on in, boys! No need for a lookout! Both scoundrels will await us in Beaver City!"

* * * *

Dick Thurman heard the shout of a voice he could not mistake, but the words it said, certainly did not fit the nature of the man shouting them. Thurman was already on his feet moving from his desk to a cabinet in the corner of his office, when yet again, the voice called out from down the street.

"Come out, NOW! You are not welcome in MY TOWN!"

Thurman picked up his pace, grabbed a double-barreled shotgun from the cabinet, insured it was loaded, dumped extra shells in his coat pocket, and darted toward the door. Had he a choice, the mayor of Beaver City would not have chosen this path. But, he'd known Elijah Smith just too long to let the fool get himself killed.

* * * *

Margaret swished the feather duster one way and then the other, not really intending to clean, but only desiring to be occupied. Moving hands often worked to quiet a far too unruly mind. Surely if she did not now apply her hands to senseless tasks, she would be employing them to pack her belongings. She did not want to think these thoughts but would have chosen a better way of brandishing them from her mind than having someone suddenly burst through the store's door at her back. Out of sheer fright, she dropped the duster, grasped at her thumping chest, and turned to see the teen Mark Frisk gasping for air.

"Young man! Have you no better sense or manners than to…"

"Your husband, Mrs. Smith!" He interrupted in a howl. "He is calling them out with rifle in hand!"

Elijah?

This made no sense and surely could not be. And neither did the emotion that came with the announcement. Margaret tore for the door, shoving Mark Frisk from her path. Elijah could not be calling out the two dangerous men in the saloon. And she could not be dreading so desperately that he might actually do such.

Margaret hit the deserted main street at a dead run, bundling the hem of her dress to keep it from slowing her down. One lone man with a rifle did, in fact, stand in the middle of the street ahead, facing

140

the Beaver City Saloon. When she drew near enough to make out the all too familiar form with the bowler on his head, she let out a wail.

Two men strolled from the saloon with pistols in both hands, but down at their sides. Another man, looking to be Dick Thurman, came at a run from the far end of the street with a shotgun at the ready. Across from the street from her, the businessman Tom Johnson raced ahead with a rifle filling his hands.

Words were exchanged between her husband and the outlaws that she could not hear.

Then Elijah abruptly raised the rifle to his shoulder.

Margaret took her last running step as fire shot from the ends of barrels, thunder erupted, and smoke filled the street. From where she stood, it appeared as if her husband took invisible punches to his torso, causing him to first stumble rearward, and then topple over backwards. As one continuous scream ripped from her lips, her peripheral vision took in Tom Johnson spinning in place, falling to his knees, and crashing over face down. Margaret made it to within just a few steps of her downed husband when she looked up to see Dick Thurman fumbling to reload the shotgun. A quick glance across the street revealed that all four of the pistols now pointed in his direction. The force of the rounds that poured into Thurman sent him sideways and through a plate glass window. All Margaret could then see were his two feet sticking out the window. Poor Dick had lost one shoe in the firestorm. Now neither the shod foot nor the bare one did as much as twitch.

Margaret fell to her knees at the side of her husband. Blood spouted from far too many holes, and he labored to breathe. Bitter laughter sounded across the street, and Tom Johnson moaned and groaned. Margaret reached, and gently took one of Elijah's hands in both of hers.

She could see that he struggled greatly to focus on her face.

"I did no good here today," he gasped.

Margaret bent, putting her face to his and soaking his cheek from the tears trickling down hers.

"Nothing could be further from the truth. You cannot *know* the good you did here today."

The hand in hers fell limp. She laid it gently upon the still chest and pushed to her feet. For a long moment she stared down at the man that she now *knew* she loved in some strange fashion. Bringing the backs of both her hands up to clear the moisture from her cheeks, she turned and walked strait and tall toward the two gunmen.

She drew as near as she cared to before stopping. It was not fear that determined the pacing but burning disgust. Both men eyed her while casually reloading their firearms. The Apache displayed a solemn expression. The buckskin clad man beside him laughed in a most obnoxious manner.

Margaret looked hard into the Apache's eyes. "Shut him up," she demanded.

The Indian mumbled something to Bemo she could not hear. Bemo shot the Apache a cold, hard look, but did reduce his merriment to a mere chuckle.

Now, Margaret deliberately moved her eyes from one man's face to the other. "You will live to regret this day," she said with not as much as a quiver in her voice. "I *will see to it* that the people of this town rip you limb from limb. What little pieces remain of you will be fed to hogs."

The Indian's only response was a narrowing of his eyelids. Bemo raised his chin to the air and cackled in delight.

"Laugh now you, fool. But, I will laugh when you no longer can," Margaret Smith turned and walk right down the middle of the street unmolested.

CHAPTER ELEVEN

Awful frame of mood

He'd long grown tired of shadowing such inept men as the ones he now left behind right after Danner shouted all Sawbuck Sam needed to know. How could any damned man associated with these parts be watched and not know he's being watched? Sawbuck Sam damn sure knew when a set of eyeballs was eyeballin' him. Although this characteristic of weakness continued to puzzle him, it made little damned difference now. The next time he laid eyes on Danner and his gang, it would be face to face, and Sawbuck would no longer feel in grave danger of doing so. Best he could recall, Beaver City, the destination shouted to the entire world by Danner, laid a two-day leisurely trip ahead. Sawbuck, however, did not intend on taking his time. The quicker he could make acquaintances with the damned men Danner hunted, the better off Sawbuck would be.

* * * *

The day had dragged long enough to feel like three. Danner, along with Abe, Walt, and Zed, sat staring into the flames of the campfire. The women lay close enough by to benefit from the heat. The men only spoke sporadically, and always on the same topic.

"I cannot help but now think of Dan Strapp, Rob Cotton, and Buzz Libby of the Four Deuces Ranch," Zed said as he finished rolling a cigarette. "The day that Laughing Billy sent them to their maker, he did it by setting a trap." Zed stuck the cigarette between his lips and put a match to it. "He will set one for us as well."

"I expect as much," Danner agreed.

"Lordy, Lordy," Abe exclaimed, "Two mens sittin' in a town jus' 'a waitin' fo five mens to come and gets 'em. Any two mens I's ever known had five mens after 'em, they'd be on da run. Done makes no sense to me."

"I have looked them both square-dabbed in the eyeballs, Abe," Zed said as he emitted a plume of smoke. "Had you ever done the same, it would make sense a plenty to you. They ain't nothin' like any two other men you have ever met…or hope to meet."

Danner glanced over at Walt to find him staring hard at the ground between the toes of his townsfolk's brogans. Suddenly, Danner felt a sense of near relief as inspiration came to him to fulfill a role that CB Wooly might play.

"Well, fellers, let us not fail to observe a fine point just made by ol' Abe here. It is in fact five against only two." To further emphasize a point, and hopefully encourage those in his charge, he turned his head to stare directly at Walt. "Not to mention that one of our five, if of a mind and a…constitution, could take on and defeat those two with no help from us other four."

Walt raised his eyes from the ground to stare into the dancing flames. "I do regret," he started speaking softly, "that it must plague you men fiercely, not knowing what, when called to action, the coward Walt Tabor will do."

Danner sought words that would neither confirm nor deny Walt's statement, when Abe came to his rescue.

"I knows what 'cha'll do, Walt. I done seen you do it. I knows dat when we needs you…you sho be der at our sides."

Walt gave Abe just the slightest smile and an appreciative nod of his head. As for Danner, he envied Abe for what he believed.

* * * *

Fannie watched as Annie prepared her bedding for their last night on the trail. She knew she should do the same, but lingered beside the waning fire on which they'd prepared their supper. Try as she might, she could not pry her mind off Floyd Danner. Had he and his men met up with the Apache and Bemo? If so, and she quaked to ponder, what had been the outcome? So deep did she dwell on the fate of the man that she nearly fell from her perch on a log when Annie thrust a rifle in her hands.

"Are you deaf?" Annie whispered as she hurriedly kicked dirt on the small flame. "A rider approaches at a gallop!"

Fannie jumped to her feet and along with her sister, aimed in the direction from which they'd traveled.

"Do not shoot ladies!" a voice called out from the dark. "It is just me, Hound Olivo!"

Hound? Her inner voice screamed. Why was he here *and why were the others not here with him?*

"Come on in, Hound," Annie shouted.

Hound came in at a trot and swung out of the saddle.

"What has happened?" Fannie all but screamed, "And where are the others?"

"All are safe, Missus Francis," Hound assured her. "We didn't meet up with the scoundrels we seek, but found two women badly in need of doctoring. Floyd asked that I find you and see if you might be willin' to travel back with me to…"

"Come, Annie. Let us hurriedly prepare our wagon for travel," Fannie ordered as she moved to do her part. Before she could reach the wagon, Hound bounded to block her path.

"Ma'am, I don't think it wise to set out tonight. I seen no trace of the Indian and Laughing Billy, and don't believe them to be in these parts, but think it best we take no chances in the dark."

Annie placed a comforting hand on Fannie's elbow. "Hound is right, sister. Let us rest tonight and start out at morning's first light."

After a moment of silent contemplation, Fannie begrudgingly gave in to the common sense of waiting until morning. "Hound, did you have your supper?"

"Had neither dinner nor supper, Ma'am. Been riding hard to reach you. I would appreciate a bite of anything you might have handy."

Busy hands could often sooth an aching mind, and Fannie felt grateful for the opportunity to prepare Hound a meal. While she began the preparations, Annie sat Hound down at the smoldering coals. She worked to rekindle a fire while assaulting Hound with a barrage of questions.

No matter how uneasy her innards, Fannie could not help but smile as she listened to her sister trying to pull answers from Hound. She might as well been trying to pull teeth from a turtle.

* * * *

"Just what I expected!" Graybow shouted into the darkness.

The mounted men in front of Martha Henry came to an abrupt stop, and she pulled hard on her reins to keep her buggy from careening into them.

"Lantern lights burn from the windows," she heard Graybow bellow.

Every muscle in her body ached from far too many hours on the road. A mile or so back she'd felt a tinge of relief when Graybow called out that his ranch lay just ahead. Any hopes of soon being in an actual bed now melted away and agitation took their place.

"What is going on up there, Graybow?" she shouted.

"Looks to be squatters, and I can most probably call them by name," he shouted back.

Martha slumped in her seat as she listened to Graybow shout orders for his men to surround the house. When the path to her front cleared, she pulled her coach forward so as not to miss the action. From just a barely safe distance to their rear, she could observe Graybow and the man they called only Bear posted on their horses. The hack Hathcoat pulled his buggy alongside, and Martha offered only a look of disgust.

"Finally, I most assuredly will have a thing of significance to pen," he called out to her.

"You should pull up closer," she responded. "God willing, you might catch a stray bullet."

As he did with all her slights and insults, Hathcoat merely chuckled.

Martha, still eying Hathcoat, jumped when two shots were fired in quick succession.

"Indian, if you're in there with that laughing fool," Graybow thundered, "come out, or we will come in. If we have to come in, I will fry you alive on a spit. But only after I gouge out your eyeballs!"

Much sooner than Martha expected, the front door opened and a frightfully skinny man in bibbed overalls stepped out waving his hands in the air.

"I ain't got no gun!" the man screamed. "I have a wife and two young 'uns inside!"

Graybow didn't immediately respond. Martha figured him puzzled by who showed over who didn't.

"And who else is in there beside your kin?" He shouted after finding his voice.

"Ain't nobody else, sir. Just my wife and young 'uns."

"Get 'em out here with you then," Graybow ordered.

Martha watched as a woman and two small and shabbily dressed children scurried out the door and huddled together in fear.

"No one else in there?" Graybow boomed.

"No sir, Mr. Graybow. This is it. Just me and my family."

"So, you know who I am? You know who you have trespassed against?"

"Oh, yes sir, Mr. Graybow. I know who you are, and you have seen me before. I am a hand for Mayor Dick Thurman in his livery stables. We only been here a little over a day, Mr. Graybow, and my wife has already been cleaning on your place, and she cleans real good. We only came here to escape the evil that has fallen upon Beaver City."

Martha observed Graybow lean forward in interest. "What evil do you speak of, trespasser?"

"Sir, my name is Joiner, Jim Joiner, but I will answer to any name you care to call me. But we meant you no offense, and thought…"

"What evil," Graybow shouted, "do you speak of, *Jim Joiner?*"

"That devilish Indian and that laughing madman, Mr. Graybow. They have sure 'nough returned to extract vengeance on the citizens of Beaver City."

So, Martha thought with a smile, the Apache and Laughing Billy Bemo were indeed in the vicinity. She was for the first time truly thrilled she chose to join this adventure.

* * * *

Danner sat alone at the fire, gazing into the embers. The others had set about settling in for the night. Sleep did not seem a possibility for him. His body felt tired, but he knew his mind would not let it rest. Occasionally, one of the women would moan, a night bird would call, and a faraway coyote would howl. Other than that, Danner wished his thinking could be as quiet as the darkness that lurked beyond the campfire.

Two capable and evil forces awaited the decisions of his active mind. What to do and how to do it plagued him to the quick. He did so anticipate the hopeful arrival of the lovely Fannie, but dreaded yet another departure to go forth and do what he wasn't yet sure how to do. Were the Apache and Bemo really in Beaver City, or did they wait in hiding on the road ahead? If they were in Beaver City, how would he make his approach? Questions pressed while answers evaded. Assuming all his men now long asleep, Danner was startled by a sudden noise to his rear. He spun, with hands on holstered pistols, to find Walt standing behind him holding the reins of his saddled mount. Danner jumped to his feet and held his arms out wide in disbelief.

"What the hell are you doing, Walt?" he hissed.

"I am leaving, Floyd," Walt said with a nod of his head.

"Why, you son of a..."

151

"But I will be back," Walt interrupted.

"Where the hell are you going?"

"I have something to do. I prefer to keep that to myself. However, I do give you my word that I'll return before you leave for Beaver City."

"Your word," Danner growled, "that is all you leave me with?"

"If you don't choose to let me go, I cannot whip you, and I would never shoot you. So, at this moment, if you do not care to whip or shoot me…I will take my leave."

Danner pulled both of the Colts, but suddenly felt just too damned tired and perplexed to point them. "Get out of here," he mumbled.

Walt swung into the saddle and looked down at Danner. "The Apache and Bemo will wait as long as it takes for you to get there. If you hold off just two days, you *will* see me again."

"Don't doubt I'll see you again" Danner spat, "but most likely it'll be in hell."

* * * *

Zed and Abe busied themselves with horse grooming as the sun continued its rise into the morning sky. Danner knew they did so as more of a comfort to themselves than as a service to the animals. They busied their hands in order to set aside their thinking. Danner wished he could do the same. He barely managed to keep wood on the fire to provide warmth for the women. Both were quiet and still, seemingly no better, but thankfully, no worse than the night before. Danner hated just sitting and waiting but knew that the day primarily held that in store for him. He longed for Hound to return with the twins in toll for the women's proper treatment and the consoling of his heart and mind.

Zed and Abe had risen with the sun nearly four hours in the past. Before they could pose questions, Danner informed them of the latest development.

"Boys, Walt Tabor has taken his leave."

Long seconds passed before Zed asked, "Where to?"

"Have no idea, Zed." Then he reluctantly added, "He asked that we wait here two days, promising that he would return in that length of time."

"You think he will, Floyd?"

Danner had not enough time to answer Zed before Abe added to the conversation.

"I bets he will. Often be my guts tells me more than my brains, and Ol' Abe's guts be sayin' he's a' comin' back."

Danner now turned his head to study Abe as he picked his horse's hooves. Still, four hours later, he wished he could put stock in the man's gut response.

The rest of the day pretty much went that way – men doing what they could to busy their hands just to keep their minds on the here and now. Abe volunteered to do what he could to clean and air out the awful little cabin. Danner appreciated the effort, knowing Annie and Fannie would need a more suitable place to doctor the women than on the ground.

Zed and Hound cleaned and oiled all the weapons, and then set about at the near impossible task of scrounging additional firewood. All along, Danner did what he could to tend to the two women. He'd continued to force small drops of water down the dark-haired woman's gullet, and she finally opened her eyes about four in the afternoon. Still, she could only draw shallows breaths of air. The blonde had managed to force down a few bites of food, but made no attempts to move from her sitting position beside the fire.

The sun didn't have too much hanging on to do when Danner heard Zed call out from a nearby field. His words set Danner's heart to racing.

"It's them, Floyd!" Zed had joyously bellowed. "Hound's back with the twins!"

* * * *

Danner ran to help Fannie down from her wagon. He gripped her in an embrace that lasted long enough he feared to prove presumptuous. If Fannie took offense, she showed no evidence of such. Annie had already climbed down by the time Danner loosened his grip on her sister. Annie walked a few feet from the wagon as her neck craned and her eyes searched. For what she longed to see, Danner had no doubt, and dreaded when questions would be asked about the whereabouts of "John Turner."

The men had all gathered around now and greetings were shared between them and the twins. Danner took Fanny by the hand and guided her to where the other women convalesced beside the fire.

Fanny and Annie knelt beside them and both fussed with checking for fevers and the rate their hearts pumped blood through their veins. "The cabin yonder was so pitiful a place that we left them here where we found them," Danner explained to the twins, "but, thanks to Abe's diligence, it is a much more suitable place to tend them now. With your instruction, Annie, we'll move them to an awaiting bed."

Annie pointed to Danner and Abe. "You each pick one up as gently as possible being sure to cradle their necks. Zed and Hound, I'll be in need of water as hot as you can manage."

Once inside the cabin that no longer evoked gagging, Abe placed the blonde on the right side of the bed and Danner laid the brunette beside her. Finding nothing resembling even partially clean bedding, Abe had covered the straw filled mattress with his and Zed's rain gear.

"Abe, would you please fetch a blanket from the box at the rear of our wagon?" Annie asked. "Once I've bathed them, I'll need it to cover them. Can't have them getting chilled."

Abe hurriedly set about the fetching with Danner purposely right on his heels. However, he made it not two feet before Annie called his name.

"Where is John?"

Danner drew in a deep breath before emitting a prepared lie. "Annie, he's out doing some scouting. Expect him back sometime tomorrow."

* * * *

If memory served him right, the way station stood only a few more miles down the badly rutted road. The first and only time he'd been there, the little inn served mostly the muleskinners responsible for the deeply cut tracks in the road. Walt Tabor had dreaded since leaving Bemo's place that this trip could possibly be all for naught. The way station could have closed down in the past year. The old man might have died, or might have not kept the promise made.

When he'd been released by CB Wooly, and so quickly escaped Beaver City, Tabor rode south, having decided Mexico a suitable destination for a man with a reputation he could not escape in the whole of the United States. No, he had not asked that CB relieve him of his responsibilities, but instead of insisting on staying, he too quickly accepted the offer made. Soon enough, the word would spread and the act of his departure would only lend credence to his well-earned and dastardly title. By the time Tabor stumbled across the way station a year or so earlier, his mood held little tolerance for foolishness.

Now, with only miles to go before reaching what he sought, Tabor's mind turned back to the evening of his first entering the establishment on the rutted road.

* * * *

It'd been a hot and dusty trip of many miles on his third day away from Beaver City when he came upon the way station with an inn and tavern. Tabor patted at the fine coating of dust that nearly covered his fancy apparel before stepping through the door of the tavern. A man well past middle-age stood behind a counter pouring drinks for a table of three loud and obnoxious muleskinners.

Just the expensive Colts Tabor wore in Mexican-looped holsters set him aside from the rough-hewn muleskinners. Had he only the fancy holsters and revolvers worn over a more frontier style of clothing, they might not have given him a second glance. It was the double-breasted vest, cotton sack coat, and the short-crowned Stetson with a wide pencil-rolled brim that turned glancing into out and out staring.

"Well, gawtdamn, fellers, I do believe Bat Masterson has joined our little party," the biggest of the three bellowed.

Tabor offered no response to the drunk as he walked up to the man behind the counter and asked for a whiskey.

"Say, Mister," the big man shouted, "Are you Bat Masterson?"

"He ain't Bat," a second man at the table chimed in. "I hunted buffalo with Masterson back in the good ol' days. He had dark hair and stood a head shorter than that dandy."

The big man turned to the only slightly smaller one at his table. "Shut your mouth, Oley, I ain't talkin' to you. Hell, I know he ain't Bat Masterson."

"Why heck, Thomas," Oley grinned, "I didn't know you didn't know it was him."

The third man then gave a showing of his wisdom. "I knew Thomas knew he wasn't him. I figured right off the get-go that Thomas was just jerking that man's reins."

"Mack, you shut your face too," Thomas ordered menacingly. "I want that man to tell me he ain't Bat Masterson even though I know he isn't. Now it's just become a matter of displaying bad manners. Hey!" Thomas shouted in Tabor's direction, "I'll ask one more time, are you Bat Masterson?"

Tabor downed his whiskey before turning to face Thomas. "I am not Bat Masterson."

"Then who are you, all gussied-up and carrying high-dollar weaponry?"

Tabor looked Thomas hard in the eyes. "I'm just a man who intends to be left alone."

Thomas shot up from the table. "You intends, so do you? Well, I intends to know your name!"

Tabor knew there was no sense in putting off what was bound to be put on. He placed the whiskey glass on the counter and stepped off in the direction of Thomas and the two others. Mack and Oley jumped up to stand alongside Thomas. Tabor whipped out both Colts, spun them in his hands to bring both up with butts forward in club-like fashion.

He waded in.

The butts of his Colts soon collided enough times on available heads to leave all three muleskinners moaning and writhing on the planked floor.

"My name is Walt Tabor, and you boys caught me in an awful frame of mood."

He then walked back to the counter and calmly asked the old proprietor for another whiskey. As the man poured with age-gnarled hands, Tabor asked him, "My name. Does it mean anything to you?"

"No, sir. Should it?"

"Not really. It's of no true significance."

Tabor downed the second whiskey before saying, "I'd like to ask you a favor, and I'll pay a fair price if you agree."

"Get to the asking," the proprietor smiled.

* * * *

Tabor reached the way station just before the sun's setting and a faint glow of lamp light shown from the windows. Now, Tabor had only to wish the old proprietor still among the living – and a man who kept his word. Tabor opened the door of the tavern and stepped in to see the old man sitting at a desk behind the counter. His name, not hard to recall, was Andrew Jackson – named after the president at the time of his birthing. Jackson looked up to see who had entered, cocked his head, and grinned.

"So, you did come back."

Tabor smiled and replied, "Truly didn't think I ever would, but here I am, Mr. Jackson."

Jackson pushed up from his desk and hobbled around the counter. "A few days after you were last in, I read the accounts of CB

Wooly's demise in Beaver City. It was only then that the name Walt Tabor meant anything to me."

"And you were disgusted for having dealings with me?" Tabor sighed.

"No, sir. I fought for the south during the war of northern aggression. We were terribly out gunned and outnumbered by the end of it, and there was more than one time I could do nothing but turn and run. And, as a result, here I stand today."

Tabor thought hard on the words for several seconds before nodding his head and saying, "And so do I."

"Will you be needing a room for the evening?"

"No, sir, but I could use a fresh horse along with the other stuff I've now got a feeling you still have on hand."

* * * *

The sun peaked over the horizon as Graybow and his men saddled their horses while the livery stable hand, Jim Joiner, scurried to ready Martha's coach and horse for the trip into Beaver City. Graybow had intended to ride in the day before, but decided the men and horses could use a day's rest. He'd declared upon the night he'd returned to his home that Joiner and his rag-tag family could sleep in his barn, and he'd feed them, for a return of services. The woman could keep the house and prepare the meals, and the man would tend the horses and do whatever menial tasks Graybow demanded.

Graybow walked his horse from the barn just as Martha descended the steps of the front porch.

"I thought maybe you decided to sleep in," he called to her.

She held a response until staring him in the face. "Sleep in? In those disgusting dust caked sheets? I have never spent a more miserable two nights and am not accustomed to such squalor."

Graybow turned away and climbed into his saddle. He had yet to lash out at the Madam Henry, but felt his patience growing thin. "The house has been abandoned for well over a year. Mrs. Joiner is making good progress and will see to the sheets and other cleaning tasks throughout the day. If you wish, you can stay here and give her a hand."

Graybow had received less vicious looks from Comanches intent on killing him, but the woman held her tongue as she stomped off toward her coach.

* * * *

Eden Ledford stood from his sitting position upon observing the lone rider approaching from town. He worked at dusting off his bottom when he recognized the man on the horse as the despicable bar owner, Rowland Beans. Ledford longed for any information about the goings-on in town but didn't care to share a single word with the big-mouthed Beans. Had the sorry no-account not told the two murderers that Ledford had a wife, the town marshal might have been provided other opportunities other than being cast from his town to serve as a lowly lookout.

Two days earlier, Ledford thought he heard the far-off sounds of gunfire. He did not know if they come from town, but feared they might. It'd taken all he possessed to keep from unhitching his horse and riding like hell back into Beaver City. Since he had not, he'd slept only winks ever since, and thought even less of himself than he did prior to hearing the sounds that might or might not have been gunfire.

At least Beans claimed enough common sense not to ride up directly where Ledford stood, but stopped a safe distance ahead.

"I fear you might still be sore at me, Marshal Ledford," Beans called out.

Ledford took deep and calming breathes, but still could not help but respond, "If murder was in me, Rowland Beans, I would shoot you right off that sorry looking horse."

"I do regret you harbor those feelings, Marshal, but at the time I told what I knew, I didn't know the consequences of my telling."

Ledford considered the words and forced a nodding of his head to accept their meaning. "Were gunshots fired the other day in Beaver City?" he asked.

"They were, but your wife is safe. No harm has come to her. Still, Elijah Smith and Dick Thurman are dead. Tom Johnson might soon be as well. The three tried to take on the Indian and the madman."

Ledford jerked the hat from his head and threw it to the ground. Three good men had attempted to do his job, and here he stood as useless as even a more despicable character than Rowland Beans, who had the good sense to simply duck his head and allow Ledford the convenience of debating his own worthlessness.

"Why are you here now?" Ledford could only mutter.

"Those two sent me to make sure you are still here. They told me not to approach or talk to you, but I figure what they don't know...then they don't know. Besides, I wanted to make my apologies. I am truly sorry, Marshal Ledford, for the role I played in you being here now."

Ledford took in a deep breath and exhaled it loudly before picking up his hat and placing it back on his head. "I guess, Rowland, that we are both truly victims of highly unusual circumstances, but please do tell who is it that I am here to look out for?"

"That would be Floyd Danner, and whoever might be riding with him. Danner was C.B. Wooly's…"

"I know who the man is, Rowland," Ledford interrupted.

Both men stood silently until a thought brightened Ledford's disposition. "Rowland, do the townsfolk know this? Do they know Danner might be coming our direction with help?"

"I doubt they do, Marshal."

"Then they need the hope, Rowland."

Ledford took a few moments to gather his thoughts and draw a conclusion. "On your way back in, can you stop off to spare a word with Margaret Smith?"

"It would be at great risk, Marshal," Beans said before pausing to do what seemed as soul searching.

"She's a strong woman, Rowland. Even though her man is dead, she would be the one to share the news of hope to others."

For the first time since riding up, Rowland Beans moved to sit straight and upright in his saddle. "Then risk be damned, Marshal. I'll make sure she knows."

* * * *

Graybow halted his party of riders and buggies one mile north of Beaver City. The squatter Joiner told Graybow that the Apache and Bemo posted a look-out south of the town, but had no knowledge of one being sent to the north. If there'd been one dispatched, Graybow would have encountered him by now. Evidently, the two hired guns felt they had no fear of anyone approaching from the north. That would mean the Apache and Bemo either did not consider Graybow's returning or did not consider him an enemy. Graybow stood prepared to deal with either possibility.

"Gather around men," he ordered from his saddle, and waited for the other five riders to pull in close.

"What we will encounter today could be as viscous as a hell storm, or as tame as a social call. I only intend to kill the Apache and that laughing bastard if they show even the slightest signs of calling for such. It might be they are not here in pursuit of me. If so, we'll let them be."

The man, even Graybow knew only as Bear, leaned forward in his saddle. "Do you propose a way of determining that before we just ride in on top of them?"

"You think I'm some kind of fool? That I don't know the business of dealing with killing types?" Graybow growled.

Bear sat back in his saddle and offered a spiteful grin. "I know you still stand to pay me a good sum of money. I just intend to be alive to collect it."

Of course, Graybow had a plan. For a second, he considered changing it so as to involve this man with the simple and singular name, but his initial motive proved stronger. He turned to the youngest of the men.

"Friday, you are going to ride in ahead of us. You will go to the Apache and Bemo in that saloon. You will tell them I'm coming. If you be standing out front when we arrive, I'll know they intend me no harm. If you be dead…be guaranteed I will avenge your death."

The "Kid" cocked his head to the side and squint his eyes at Graybow. "I consider that a fairly raw deal."

"Yeah, well, it is the hand you've been dealt. So, play it," Graybow squinted back.

Kid Friday seemed to think it over before responding with a cocky grin. "I'll play it. But when you get there and they are both dead, and I'm still standing…I'll demand extra pay."

Without waiting for a response, Friday spurred his horse and took off in a trot. Graybow admired the boy's spunk. Truth was, he just didn't like the way the young lad seemed to increasingly attract a lustful eye from the Madam Henry.

CHAPTER TWELVE

Damn Sure Dying

Friday kept his horse at a walk as he made his way down the main street of Beaver City. He could feel the look of eyes watching him from shuddered windows and from behind closed curtains. But those who hid behind such did not concern him. Friday kept his eyes trained straight ahead for the destination that held the only two people in the town who did.

Friday reigned to a stop a good fifteen paces in front of the open doors to the Beaver City Saloon. Flickering lights from ceiling lamps illuminated the interior but didn't reveal any living forms. He dropped his gun hand from the reins and rested it on his lap just inches from his revolver.

"My name is Jack Friday," he called toward the opening. "I've been sent here by Stew Graybow."

Long seconds followed before a man clad in black finery stepped into view and strode casually to stand in the doorway. Both of his hands rested easily upon holstered pistols warn in cross-draw fashion.

"Hello, Jack Friday," the dark-complexioned man wearing braids and a bowler said in a calm manner. "Graybow evidently intends no harm, or he would have sent more than a mere boy."

Friday ignored the comment, figuring the laughing man stood within the shadows with him in his gun sights. "You're right in that he means no harm to you or your friend. He just wants to know that you're feeling the same."

"I have no friend," the Apache snarled. "Only an accomplice."

"Makes no difference to me either way," Friday grinned, "but Graybow will be here any minute with four other hired guns."

The Apache simply nodded his head before turning it to call over his right shoulder, "Come out here, Laughing Billy, and meet the hired gun, Jack Friday."

A high-pitched cackling preceded the appearance of a man wearing buckskins with revolvers dangling in both hands down alongside his legs. Shoulder-length blond hair fell from a hat with the front of the brim turned upward.

"Why hell, Mr. Friday," Bemo giggled, "You're about the age I was when I started toting my guns for money."

Friday just nodded his head at the comment. Then said, "So, do you mean to do harm to Graybow, me, or the others?"

"Jack Friday, if I meant to do you harm, you'd already be dead," the Apache replied.

"Yup, be done waltzing with the devil, young'un," Bemo laughed. "Besides that fact, why does the old codger think we'd be holdin' any kind of grudge against him? Hell, he put us on our horses and helped us to safety after the fight with CB Wooly."

Friday turned his head to the left at the sound of fast approaching horses. "Guess you can ask him that yourself."

* * * *

Graybow felt mixed emotions on observing Kid Friday still pulling in and letting out air – relieved that the two killers evidently hadn't come to Beaver City for him, and disappointed they hadn't put multiple rounds of hot lead in Friday. Now, the Kid would most likely be even more appealing to the Madam Henry for the brave manner in which he possibly parlayed some kind of peace with the Apache and Bemo.

Graybow pulled his horse up alongside Friday's and nodded at the Apache before saying, "Not sure what kind of mood I'd find you in, Indian."

The Apache cocked his head and squinted his eyelids before responding, "My mood seldom fluctuates, old white man."

The long-haired idiot bellowed out laughter. Graybow ignored it, and instead glanced at his men as they positioned themselves to cover his flanks. "Why have you come back to Beaver City, John Paul? Is there a bounty on my head that you'd be intending to collect?"

"Even though it is none of your business, Graybow, I'm here because it is here that the one called Danner expects to find me."

"And how do you know that?" Graybow asked.

"If I told you, you would not understand. Your lack of understanding might possibly lead to ridicule, which would result in your dying. So, best you not know how I know. However, he will come here. Whether he comes alone, or with an entire army, that I do not know."

Graybow mulled for seconds the confounding statement before responding. "Well, if he's coming here for you, then he'll be coming for me. I'd be willing to join forces if you'd be in agreement."

The Apache's answer came quickly, "No. I intend to put him down myself with the assistance of only Laughing Billy."

Graybow nodded his head. Just as well, he thought. If Danner did come with an army, or more likely a posse, Graybow could do worse than having the Apache and Bemo posted to no doubt reduce whatever force Danner might yield.

"In that case, I'll await at my ranch what might come. If you…

Graybow's hands shot involuntarily to his eyes as a spray of what felt like thick warm coffee suddenly coated his face. The shocking sensation had been preceded by a thud sounding similar to an axe blade colliding with wood, and followed by the repeat of a powerful rifle. Bear's heavy body first collapsed over the horn of his saddle and then fell to the ground. Graybow had cleared enough of the gunk from his eyes to see that it'd came from what had once been Bear's head.

The rifle sounded again, and pandemonium ruled. The Apache and Bemo shot back into the Saloon. Horses reared and spun, and out the corner of his eye, Graybow saw another of his men fly from a saddle.

"Ambush!" he thundered. "Ride for the ranch!"

Martha Henry was just pulling into sight on the far end of main street. Graybow bared down on her in a gallop and didn't pull back on his reigns until feet from colliding with her rig.

"You take the time to turn that buggy around and you might catch a stray round. I suggest you jump on with me. If you don't, you're on your own."

It both surprised and delighted Graybow when the woman climbed on behind him without saying a single word of objection or disgust.

* * * *

"How the hell they get past that marshal?" Bemo squealed with laughter.

The Apache didn't offer an immediate response. He wasn't sure there was a "they." Both shots fired came from only one gun.

"I believe it was another town citizen. I feared the stand taken by the others would encourage such foolishness."

"He might be foolish," Bemo giggled, "but not a bad shot. Dropped two of Graybow's men with led to the noggin."

The Apache nodded his head, then slowly started toward the door with a gun in each hand.

"Looks like you thinkin' on takin' a peek, JP. Not such a smart thing for such a smart feller to do. I'm bettin' that rifle has a bead on the door and just…"

"Hey Apache and Laughing Man," a voice boomed from out in the street. "I mean neither of you harm. As a matter of truth, I came to help you."

"Who are you?" the Apache called out.

"Well, now, that's going to take some damned explaining. For now, you can call me Sawbuck. I'm holding my rifle high over my damned head. Will you permit me to enter the tavern?"

The Apache backed further into the interior before giving his reply. "Move into position so that you can been seen."

Seconds later, a large and older man stepped into view with a Sharps rifle in fact held high overhead.

The Apache walked to the doorway with both pistols pointed. "Why did you open fire on those men?"

"Damned sure looked like hostiles to me. I feared they meant you and the laughing man harm. I fired for your continued good health."

The Apache lowered his pistols to his sides. "You can do the same, but do it slowly."

Sam lowered his rifle until the barrel was pointed at the ground.

Bemo stepped up to stand alongside the Apache and snickered, "You said you came to help us. Help us with what, old man?"

"There's a man named Danner headed this way with four other men. They intend to kill the both of you."

"Why would that be a concern of yours?" The Apache asked.

"Why, I had my own damned run in with Danner and his crew. They intend to kill me as well. I damned sure figured three stood a better chance against five instead of two, and a damned sure didn't like the odds of one against five."

The Apache studied Sam for long seconds before turning to Bemo. "What do you think, Laughing Billy? Is this old white man telling us the truth?"

Bemo enjoyed a bout of laughter before replying, "Well, he has told us more than we knew. Danner has four others with him. To top that, there's two fellers out there leaking brains that he thought meant us no good. He might be worth a little trusting just for that sake alone, JP."

"Is that what I'm to call you?" Sawbuck piped up. "JP?"

The Apache turned his coldest stare on him. "Do, and I will gut you."

"Well, then, do you mind if I take the revolvers from the two I dropped. Damned sure the spoils of war that I certainly deserve."

"Have at 'em," Bemo tittered.

The Apache had of yet holstered his pistols, and neither had Bemo. He watched as the big man with the long dingy gray beard laid the Sharps aside and gathered a pistol a piece from the two dead men. The Apache kept alert eyes on Sawbuck as he started their way, fumbling with attempts of stuffing the pistols in a wide belt around his ample waist.

Then both pistols came upward and took aim.

"You both drop those damned guns in your hands. I can't miss from this distance."

The Apache counted on Bemo doing exactly what the Apache did in a wink of an eye, and Bemo did. The four pistols in their hands came up and started laying down lead. When the smoke cleared, Sawbuck lay sprawled on his back in the street.

The victors remained in place, and Bemo let out a cackle when Sawbuck raised his head from the ground.

"Damn. Didn't get off a single damned round."

Bemo raised the gun in his right hand and took aim.

"Wait," the Apache ordered, "I have further use of this foolish white man." He moved to stand over Sawbuck, and reached down to retrieve a formidable knife from the old man's wide belt. Sawbuck, groaned as he let his head fall back to the hard-packed dirt of the street.

"You came here to kill us. Did Floyd send you?" the Apache asked.

Sawbuck barely shook his dead. "No. Did so on my own," he moaned, "In an attempt to gain Floyd's good graces. How many damned bullets do I have in me?"

The Apache looked him over. "Four. One in each leg. One in your shoulder, and one that most likely severed your guts."

"I'm damn sure dying," Sawbuck said pitifully.

"Hopefully, not before you serve a purpose," the Apache replied. Then he turned his head toward the saloon's open door, "Rowland Beans! Get out here," he shouted.

Beans came at a run. "Yes, sir, Mr. Apache?"

"Down the street, Graybow left behind a readied coach. Bring it here."

Beans again took off in a dash, and the Apache bent to put Sawbuck's knife to work.

* * * *

It had been a day Danner would choose to live over and over the rest of his life. Just being in the presence of Fannie Francis soothed all that beckoned for his attention. The way she spoke, the words she chose, the way she looked and smiled and moved, let him put aside the questions and doubts and fears. He *would* choose to live the day over and over if it was a choice he could make. However, it wasn't. Because the questions still needed answers, and the doubts and fears would still demand a reckoning for the deed that lay ahead.

However, even Abe, Zed, and Hound had seemed to benefit from the time spent around the twins. Abe's trepidation with being overly friendly with white women, and the cowboy's discomfort for being with "respectable" women, had all seemed to subside. Cheerful comments and light-hearted joshing became more common place with each passing hour. Danner sensed that if providence provided and time permitted, that him and these three men would nurture friendships among themselves that would last long lifetimes.

Wishful thinking.

Foolish thinking.

Had Fannie not approached him at this very moment, the day of bliss might have dissolved to anguish.

"You seem deep in thought. Hope I am not intruding."

Danner felt his solemn expression turn miraculously to glee. "Foremost, I am more than honored you consider me capable of deep thought, and if you are an intruder, I stand ready for total capitulation."

Fannie reached with her hands to take both of Floyd's and prompted him to stand from his seated position at the back of her buckboard. "And what if I demand a siege before capitulation?" she asked with a taunting smile.

"Well, my dear lady, in that you have already laid siege to my heart, soul, and mind, what else is left?"

"Look around, Mr. Danner. We are alone for the first time this day. Would you find me lacking in decorum if I desired to lay siege to your lips?"

At the risk of his knees buckling, Danner pulled Fannie into his arms and whispered in her ear, "Let decorum be damned!" His heart surely expanded three times its normal size when his lips found hers, and for mere seconds everything in him and all around him turned to heaven – mere seconds before the sounding of an approaching horse.

* * * *

Tabor rode in at a trot not expecting the joyous calling of his name by Zed, Abe, and even the typically unexcitable Hound Olivo. The greetings soothed his case of nerves brought on by the spotting of the twins' buckboard while still far away from the cabin.

Abe ran up and took charge of the horses reins to lead Tabor right up to the cabin like a paige might do for a knight returning from battle. "I done tol' em' all yous be comin' back!" he beamed, "And Lordy, Lordy, just look at ya now, all duded up like Ol' Wild Bill his ownself!"

Zed and Hound gathered close to the horse with one on each side and they patted both the horse's rump and Tabor's back.

"Returned on even a fancier horse," Hound grinned.

"Why, hell, Hound," Zed laughed, "Can't dress like that and ride a hag!"

Floyd Danner proved to be the only man that didn't seem thrilled to see Tabor again. He'd walked up with his arm around Fanny's waist and seemed just downright perturbed that he'd ridden in. Tabor surely didn't expect Floyd to act with the same enthusiasm as the others, but surely hadn't expected a scowl. At least Fanny's lovely face was beaming and her greetings nearly matched that given by the men. Tabor both longed for and dreaded to see the other lovely face on Annie Francis. Explanations would be expected of his absence, return, and manner of dress.

He only had to wait moments before Annie burst from the cabin in a near out and out run. Hound backed up so Tabor could swing out of the saddle. Without prior consideration of doing so, Tabor swooped Annie into his arms and gave her a twirl-about. Of the many ways she could have reacted, Annie chose to grace Tabor with a giggle and an enthusiastic hug. Once he lowered her to her feat, she immediately started examining his apparel with an astonished look in her gorgeous eyes.

"My, my, John Turner, you are so handsomely dressed, but why are you adorned in so extravagant attire?"

Tabor sucked in a gulp of air, held it until his lungs felt the burn, then let it slowly out through his mouth. "Annie, I've a confession to make to you and your sister that pains me so just to utter. My name is not John Turner. Truth is…I'm the *infamous coward,* Walt Tabor."

Annie's expression immediately reflected both shock and pain. "You…You lied to me." She slowly glanced into the faces of the other men. "You all lied to me." She then dropped her eyes to the ground, turned, and walked slowly back into the cabin.

* * * *

"Damn, Walt, I don't think Fannie is happy with me at the moment either. After all, it was I who introduced the lie."

As a matter of fact, she'd pulled away from Danner and strode quickly into the cabin to no doubt lend comfort to her sister. The other men quickly dispersed, and Floyd had taken Tabor by the crook of the arm to lead him away from the cabin.

"It had to be told, Floyd, and I don't know how else I could have told it. Besides, you were clearly not pleased to see me make it back and nothing I'd done would have prevented the ire you now exhibit."

"My actions at the moment of your return had only to do with the timing of your return, Walt."

"What does that mean?"

"Doesn't matter what it means. The only thing that matters now, Walt, is…you kept your word…I'm greatly appreciative that you did."

Danner first toed at the dry and dusty ground with a boot before slowly raising and offering his right hand to Danner. "We've a lot to put behind us. I'll now do my best to make that happen."

Walt took Danner's hand and gave it a vigorous shaking.

"That leaves us only to discuss our departure, Walt. I don't know how far or long you've ridden, but if you be up to it, I'd prefer to leave at first light tomorrow. The sooner we get this thing done, the better I'll be with doing it."

"The sun is not far from sinking, Floyd. I'll turn in early, and will be ready at first light."

Walt turned and took steps for his horse before Danner called again his name.

"Walt?"

"Yeah, Floyd?"

"The way you're dressed."

"What about it, Floyd?" Walt sighed.

"That's the reason you left?"

"Yeah, Floyd. Had all this stashed. Wanted it back."

Danner slowly started to nod his head, and gave the other man a sincere smile. "Glad you did. Your manner of dress now matches your abilities. Does my heart good."

Walt nodded and smiled as well before striding off to tend to his horse.

* * * *

Danner stood at the cabin door a few seconds before tapping lightly. He expected not a happy woman to answer the knock, but was more than elated when Fannie opened the door and presented him with a pleasant look of curiosity. Not exactly a smile, but not either a cold "What do you want?"

"Fannie, the boys have prepared a light evening meal of beans and cornbread if you and Annie wish to join us."

"Thank you, Floyd, but we supped earlier with Deborah and Marge. However, we would like to talk with you and uh…Walt…if you can spare the time."

"We can, and I'll go fetch him."

"You can enter without knocking, but please be quiet. The women are sleeping peacefully."

Moments later, Floyd returned with Tabor in tow.

"Should I assume hostility, Floyd?" Tabor asked before they entered.

"Fannie was pleasant enough, but, as far as I know, Annie might be out for blood."

"Thanks, Floyd," Walt mumbled.

"You're most welcome," Floyd grinned.

When they entered, both were greeted by pleasant smiles from both women.

"Although we are both victims of deceit," Fannie started right in, "We have decided that pending circumstances does not allow us the privilege of hurt feelings or anger. We both just ask that we never again be lied to in any fashion by either of you. We are strong women, and can always tolerate the truth no matter how…seemingly horrific…the truth might be."

"You have a promise from me, from here on, to be nothing but brutally honest," Danner inserted.

Tabor moved slowly closer to Annie. "And I make you the same promise, Annie."

"That being the case," Fannie said lively, "Floyd, I would ask that you follow me out so we might finish what we started just as Walt rode up."

* * * *

Tabor now understood Danner's initial scowling and the later comment made on timing. He and Fannie had just started something that needed finishing. What that was, Tabor could not be bothered with at the presence, in that he found himself alone in the main room of the cabin with Annie. The door to the one bedroom, where the other women now slept, was closed. Tabor would have felt somewhat more at ease if it stood open.

Annie was seated at the table. Tabor drew up a chair and sat beside her, folding his hands on the table in front of him. "Might as well ask without hesitation, Annie…were you more bothered by the deception…or the truth of my identity?"

For terribly long seconds, Annie just stared deeply into his eyes as if studying his soul. Then she brought up a hand from beneath the table and placed it on top of Tabor's.

"The first time I allowed myself to look deep into your eyes, Walt, I saw a sweet and kind man of tender conscience. I now see him there yet. Your name does not matter, nor what that name might mean to others. I do not fault you for decisions you made because of dire consequences of not making such decisions. I would rather have you here alive now with a taunted reputation, than being a dead man I'd never the opportunity to fall in love with."

Tabor felt his heart suddenly capable of setting fire to the rest of his body causing it to melt and puddle on the hard-packed dirt floor. "You…love me?

"I do, and only spring it on you now because of your task that lies ahead. I could not have you leaving here without knowing it. I hope only you feel something similar for me."

Tabor slipped from the chair to take a knee before Annie. "I have since first seeing your face. When I return, Annie, will you be my wife?"

Annie simply replied, "I will."

* * * *

He'd heard yet more gunfire earlier in the day, and it had been during the daylight hours that Marshal Eden Ledford made up his mind. He could no longer stand and do nothing. He'd done that far too long, leaving himself with not a thread of dignity. Now that darkness had fallen, he would saddle his horse and ride into Beaver

City. Hoping for the element of surprise, he would enter Rowland Beans' establishment with guns blazing.

If lucky, he hoped to best both the Apache and Billy Bemo, leaving them no opportunity of living. If very lucky, he would walk away unscathed and straight to his house where he intended to load up his wife, a few belongings, and leave the town and people he'd sorely neglected to protect. He prayed to do so without having to look a single citizen in the eye.

Ledford only had left to cinch tight his saddle and bridle his horse when he heard approaching riders. The fire he'd built lit only his immediate area and left all outside the small circle of light black as pitch. In a matter of seconds, he found himself surrounded by three men he did not know who now held him at gun point.

"Are you Marshal Eden Ledford?" One man asked harshly.

No longer worthy of the title, Eden responded, "I am Eden Ledford."

All three men cocked hammers, and then pulled triggers. Ledford felt the impact of three bullets, and then felt nothing ever again.

CHAPTER THIRTEEN

That's My Vision

Early morning, but the sun had not yet risen. Too early for them to be out there, but they were. He did not hear them, because they hadn't made a sound. He didn't need to hear them to know they were there. At first, they always surprised him, but he'd learned to feel their presence.

"Indian! Come out of that saloon. Step into the street," the voice of the one he knew abruptly called.

"You can come out, or we're coming in for you," the one he never met hollered. "Either way, you know how this ends."

He did. The Apache took the time to make sure his pistols were fully loaded. He placed them back in their holsters and called for his accomplice.

"Laughing Billy, they're out there. Ready your guns."

Bemo did not respond. Not even with laughter. The Apache started for the door of the saloon. Inside was cramped. Plenty of space out there. More room to maneuver. Just inside the door his eyes found Bemo lying on the floor, and Bemo started talking, but his words were not framed with laughter.

"My legs. They won't move. My legs. They won't move. My legs…"

Over and Over and Over.

The Apache threw open the front doors and called out to the men in the street. "I'm coming out, but I do not wish to fight."

A new tactic. In the other dreams of the men who haunted his sleep, he'd always chose to fight, and the result was always the same. The bullets they fired hurt more than real bullets because they were the only kind of bullets that could kill the Apache. The new tactic would work because they were lawmen. They had to follow the law. They could not shoot if he surrendered.

The Apache stepped into the street with his hands over his head.

"Well, look at that, Clay, he wants to surrender."

"He doesn't get to surrender, CB."

The Apache dropped his arms and pulled his guns before the lawmen pulled theirs, but it didn't matter. The Apache's bullets passed right through them, and when they returned fire, their magic bullets found their way to and into and all through his body like shards of hell and chunks of brimstone.

* * * *

"The men are all saddled up and ready to go." Danner could not keep his words from sounding as heavy as his heart felt. Annie was out standing beside Tabor's horse, leaving Danner and Fannie the privacy of the cabin's main room to say their goodbyes.

It'd been decided that the Francis twins would remain with Debbie and Marge until the business in Beaver City was concluded. It went unsaid, but understood, they would remain there until all who could return did return, and if none did, until the two ailing women could make it on their own. Danner had said earlier, "It should not take us longer than a week to do what has to be done."

Now, Danner and Fannie stood in an embrace. "You've not mentioned it, Fannie, but guessing you know that Walt and Annie are to be married upon his return."

If only it is meant to be.

"She told me, and I am highly pleased for her."

Danner cleared his throat. "It's certainly pleasing at that…would be only fitting…the way I see it…that it be a double ceremony. I mean…"

"Floyd Danner!" Fannie nearly squealed as she pulled her head away from his, "Are you asking me to be your wife?"

"I am if you'll have me."

This time Annie did squeal, "I'll have you!"

They sealed the arrangement with long and passionate kissing until Danner reluctantly pulled away.

"I'll not be saying good-bye, Fannie. I'm just going to walk out that door for this is not good bye, because before you know it, I'll be waking back through that door."

If only it is meant to be.

* * * *

Stew Graybow was down to Pink Corning, Tim Swonger, and Kid Jack Friday. The night before he'd sent them through Beaver City on a threefold mission. Graybow wanted to know who killed Bear and Bodie Bowman in front of the Beaver City Saloon, he wanted to retrieve Martha Henry's coach and horse, and finally he wanted to make sure no warrants would be served for his arrest.

After crawling from his bed and descending the staircase, Graybow found Corning at the kitchen table sipping on coffee. Graybow poured himself a cup and sat down across from Corning.

"How did it go last night?" Graybow asked.

"Not as good as you want to hear, but what we hired on for…killing…we got that done."

"Who fired upon us, killing Bear and Bowman?"

"Being as late as it was, we came only upon three men in Beaver City. One said he was an old man. Another said he was a trapper, and the third had no knowledge of who'd done the shooting. First man did tell that whoever he was, he ain't no more. The Apache and Bemo killed him."

Graybow scratched at his beard and took a gulp of coffee before saying, "An old trapper killed by Apache and Bemo. Don't really tell me much does it?"

"That's a fact. It does not. You'll be even less happy knowing the Madam's rig was nowhere to be seen, and the three men had nothing to shed on the fact of where it went."

"Believe I'll put off telling Miss Henry as long as possible. She'll be highly displeased."

"I reckon she will be that," Corning grinned.

Graybow didn't like it that one of his subordinates found humor in the fact that he'd surely endure a berating from the woman. "Did you all put a round in that Marshal as I ordered you to do?"

"We did," Cornish said as he stood and stretched. "Long night, boss. Got back about two hours ago. Going to get a little shut-eye."

"One more thing before you do," Graybow grumbled. "And tell the other two. Don't want the killing of that Marshal mentioned to Hathcoat. Just not something he needs to hear about."

Corning nodded his head. "Will make sure the others know, Mr. Graybow."

* * * *

It been a long and dismal day on the road. On the previous days spent mostly in the saddle, the men, not including Hound, would chatter among themselves just to while away the boredom. Today, all had been more like Hound, keeping their thoughts mainly to themselves. There'd been no tall-tales, no joking and joshing with each other, and therefore, no laughter.

Danner reckoned it just the ways of men, not by nature the killing types, who found themselves on a mission to most likely kill or be killed. As for himself, he'd been just as inward thinking as the rest. Of course, the woman he'd left behind occupied much of his thinking and certainly didn't put him in the mood to converse with anyone but her. Still, he had to admit, the lion's share of his thinking was on the Apache and Bemo. Just more on what had to be done, and even more on how to get it done. Danner wondered what he'd give to have just three minutes of conversation with CB Wooly before he entered Beaver City, and what he wouldn't give up to have both CB Wooly and Clay Bardoe at his side when confronting the Apache and Bemo.

Quickly, as he scanned his eyes over the men riding with him, he admonished himself to put such foolish thinking aside in order to consider the abilities of those who'd actually be at his side. Abe and Hound had fought the Comanche, and though neither bragged on such, Danner assumed they'd killed their fair share. Both were cool headed, calm in their mannerisms and would prove worthy under fire. Zed Martin wore a revolver and carried a Remington in his scabbard. If guessing, Danner would bet both firearms had been used for nothing more than cowboy type work – sending a rattler on its way, or maybe putting down a lame horse. Danner would be greatly surprised if Zed had ever faced another man with a gun, and would again bet he'd never fired a shot at another human being. However, if Zed were not a courageous man, he'd not be with them now. That also spoke of loyalty – a quality in which Danner considered priceless. He truly didn't know how much help Zed would be, but figured the last thing he'd do was run.

Which brought naturally to mind the fourth of Danner's party. Other than maybe Clay Bardoe, Danner had never known a man more proficient with firearms than Walt Tabor. If only Tabor had the fortitude of a Clay Bardoe, Danner would have no worries whatsoever. What Tabor would do when time came to face the two killers in Beaver City was anybody's guess. Danner could only take satisfaction in one fact he'd learned on this venture with Walt Tabor – *the man did not want to be a coward.*

Still, when it came right down to it, Danner could not help but believe it would be only himself, Abe, Hound, and Zed to take the stand against the Apache and Bemo.

* * * *

Martha Henry came downstairs late afternoon to find Graybow, Hathcoat, Corning, and Swonger playing poker at the dining room table. This interested Henry in only one respect – where was the young man not playing poker? She strolled on through the house and onto the expansive front porch. When she did not find Kid Friday there, she knew he could only be in his room or in the barn. It would not be safe checking his room at this hour, so she strolled to the barn and there found her intended prey grooming his horse. So as not to startle him, she called from the barn door.

"Mr. Friday, I'm inclined to believe you prefer the company of horses over that of people."

Friday gave her a weary looking once over before responding, "Horses tend to be less bothersome than people."

She sashayed closer to the handsome youngster. "Could you tolerate just a moment's bother from a lonely lady?" she asked in a tone that seldom failed to prick the curiosity of a man.

"I might be able to tolerate only a moment depending on your intentions."

She could tell Friday didn't trust her, but sensed that was a luxury he afforded few if any. Which, made him just that greater of a trophy.

"I'm interested in hearing about how you killed the marshal last night," she drew with a coy smile.

"I killed him with two others. Nothing to brag about."

"You found the execution distasteful then?"

"Let's just say I'd preferred something being more of a challenge."

"You clearly don't see eye to eye on much that Graybow demands of you."

"I'm just working for a paycheck, lady."

"Would you be willing to work for additional incentives?"

Friday laid aside the curry brush he employed and stepped up close to Henry. "What kind of incentives?"

Henry tilted her face to look him in the eyes. "I'd like you to come up to my room later this evening."

Friday chuckled without displaying humor. "And why would I do that?"

"To get back at Graybow for the demeaning treatment he has bestowed upon you from the onset of this *adventure*."

Friday picked up the brush and started back to work on his horse. "What time you want me there?"

* * * *

Supper around the campfire started as cheerless as the day's ride. Hound had bagged a small doe right after they'd selected a spot along the road to call it a day. Abe had helped Hound skin and butcher the deer and the meal it provided should have brought smiles to everyone's faces. Danner decided it was high time for a little levity.

"Hound and Abe, this is one fine meal you've provided, and I for one am not going to consume it like it's my last darn meal."

"Last meal?" Tabor questioned.

"Hell, yes, Walt. Here we all sit, just like we set our horses today, as if we've already ridden into Beaver City and got our asses blown clear off. As of yet, I'm not dead, and I'm not going to act that way any longer. Anyone else caring to come to life just join in at any moment."

For a split second, Danner thought he'd plum over motivated Zed Martin, for Zed shot upright from his seated position, brought his arms up to flay over his head and literally started dancing a jig. The look on his face was not one of contagious joy but instead, stark terror.

"A SPIDER! SPIDER DOWN MY SHIRT! JEEESUSSS CHRIST A SPIDER DONE CRAWLING DOWN MY BACK!"

Danner figured every other man wished to help Zed as much as he did. However, all others were laughing almost as hardily. Danner and Abe were completely bent at the mid-section and gasping for air. Tabor looked not much better off, and even Hound, who might have chuckled a couple of times in his life was now guffawing. After gyrating in and amongst the others for several seconds, Zed simply launched himself in the air and came down flat on his back. For long moments he just laid there, but did finally make an announcement.

"I think I squished it."

Hound made his apologies first. "Sorry, Zed, couldn't help but laugh. I've seen hoochie-coochie girls who couldn't dance near that enthusiastically."

Danner followed suit. "Yep, sorry Zed. I've known cowboys that feared snakes, thunderstorms, and swollen rivers, but never seen one put such emphasis into a dislike."

"I's thinkin' the devil done took holt 'cha...guess that ain't no thing to laughs about," Abe added.

Zed sat upright. "Spiders are from the devil, Abe. You 'uns get bit by the right spider in the right place, you'd be knowing it true."

All continued to josh and laugh, and eventually Zed even started to chuckle. The merriment, however, came to an abrupt stop at the sound of a horse and wagon wheels on rough footing followed by a faint plea for help.

* * * *

Graybow had looked beyond his hand of cards to watch the Madam Henry making her way up the stairs. Not fifteen minutes later, he observed Kid Friday doing the same. He didn't finish the hand he'd been dealt before the awful possibility came to mind. Graybow dropped the cards, stood abruptly, and bolted for the stairs.

He didn't bother knocking or even turning the door handle to the Madam's room. He kicked the door open, and as he suspected, tangled in her sheets was the Madam and the Kid.

"You son of a bitch!" Graybow thundered as he grabbed for the revolver stuck down the front of his trousers. Before he could jerk it free, the Kid rolled to his side and grabbed a gun from the nightstand.

"Stand easy, old man," he hissed as he cocked and took aim.

"You son of a bitch!" He shouted with even more intensity and then turned his glaring eyes on the Madam. "You! You…WHORE!"

Martha chuckled as she said, "You just figuring that out, Graybow?"

"By God, you both leave here right now, and you," Graybow pointed at Friday, "will leave without pay."

Friday shook his head and grinned. "I won't speak for the Madam, but I ain't going anyplace. Whether you like it or not, Graybow, you need me. I will be staying until this job is through and I draw every cent of my wages."

"I'm here to see it through as well, Graybow, and I'm damned sure not leaving without my coach."

Graybow gave them the nastiest look he could muster. "Corning and Swonger will see to you both leaving."

"Don't think you'll find either willing to lift a finger, Graybow," Friday chuckled. "They'll admit what you won't. Men are coming. They need me. You need me."

"The Kid's right, Mr. Graybow," Corning's voice sounded from behind Graybow.

He wheeled about to find that not only Corning, but Swonger and Hathcoat had jointed him on the second floor of the house.

"Are you saying you'll disobey my orders, Corning?" Graybow hissed.

"I'm saying, Mr. Graybow, that if the Kid goes, me and Swonger go with him. We don't know how many men might be coming for you, but we're betting there'll be more than two. Without the Kid, we don't like the odds."

For nearly fifty years, Graybow had employed men. For that long, he'd given orders – and insured they were carried out. He'd had men buck-up in the past, refusing to do as told, but only momentarily. In those days he couldn't have found a man to hire that he couldn't out fight or out shoot. In a situation like he now faced, he'd jumped in with fist, teeth, and feet, and he wouldn't have lost. Those times as well as those abilities were well past, and now he found himself for the first time in company with those he could not out fight or out shoot. The least he'd suffer for taking on these men would be an ass whipping.

Beaten without even a fight, Graybow turned to go, but not before growling at the author Hathcoat, "Do not you dare pen a word of what happened here this day."

* * * *

The second encounter with the man seemed as strange to all as the first encounter, when they'd found him naked in the middle of the road. This time Sawbuck Sam had his clothing, but was barely alive and in a luxurious coach pulled by a particularly fine horse.

Danner had to lean close to make out the old man's muttering.

"Fought to stay alive. Had to get to you with their damned message." He then held up both hands to reveal that the thumb and index finger of both had been brutally chopped away. "So's I can never cock or fire another firearm," he moaned. "Not even, the damned Indian said, when I meet him again in hell."

Blood and puss oozed from numerous wounds that looked like bullet holes to Danner. "The Apache did you this grievous harm, Sam?"

The old warrior seemed only minutes from death and barely got out, "Yes, and the other man you seek. Thought I could kill them for you. Making amends for the boys."

Tabor stepped up close. "What message do you have for us, Sam?"

Danner winced at the asking, knowing whatever message they sent would not be good for his men to hear. "Sawbuck, don't talk. Save your breath."

Sawbuck managed to barely shake his head. "Said they'd do damned worse to you fellers than they did to me."

By the light of a half-moon, Zed and Abe dug a grave. Danner, with the help of Hound, moved the heavy body from the coach to the shallow hole. All along, Walt Tabor stood several paces away with his back turned to the others.

* * * *

Bemo sat on a bar stool and cackled as he slapped both knees. "Damn, JP, if you don't just beat all. You tell me, all serious like, that your blamed vision has changed once again, but you never tell me what this *vision* is all about in the first place."

"I do not care for you to ridicule what is sacred to me," the Apache mumbled as he paced in front of the bar to the Beaver City Saloon.

"Ridicule? Thinkin' that means poking fun at you, Indian. Now, what makes you think I'd ever do something like that? Hell, the sun's not even up. Too early for me to be joshing about anything." Bemo giggled.

The Apache leveled his eyes on Bemo, and nodded his head knowingly. Rowland Beans was still upstairs, and would not hear if the Apache now cared to share his vision.

"If you were to *poke fun* at my vision, I would not be responsible for my actions."

"All right," Bemo laughed heartedly, "I'll give you my word not to offend you, if only you will tell me about the damned vision."

The Apache silently considered the offer for several seconds. Bemo knew he couldn't kill him, but Bemo didn't know that he might not lose at least one ear if he failed to keep his word.

"Two dead men appear in my vision. One we both met…CB Wooly. The other we are acquainted with by only the tales we've heard told…Clay Bardoe. They have appeared to me wherever I might be. Now, they appear here in Beaver City. We always fight, and they always win because they are no longer from this world.

"Last night, when they appeared, the two became one man who was forced to take back his human nature and vulnerabilities. He could be killed, but before I could kill him, he reached into my chest and took away my heart."

The Apache strolled around the end of the bar and poured him a stout whiskey, took a hearty swig, and said not another word.

"That's it?" Bemo snickered. "That's all you have to tell me?"

"That's my vision."

"Why, hell, don't make no sense to me. What does it mean?"

The Apache downed the rest of the whiskey. "My heart has become my Achilles' heel. Among Danner's party will come a man with both the qualities of both CB Wooly and Clay Bardoe. If he can put a bullet in my heart, I will surely die."

Bemo laughed a laugh that showed no enthusiasm. "Now, I don't know what hill you'd be talking about in these parts, but you've left me clear out of this here picture, JP. I'll be doing my part to make sure you take no bullets to the heart."

The Apache let his concern show in a slow shaking of his head. "I do fear you will be of no help, Laughing Billy. When the time comes, your legs will no longer work."

* * * *

The sun was just peaking over the horizon when Danner felt a hand tugging on his arm that quickly prompted him to sit upright on his bedroll.

"What is it, Hound?"

"Tabor," Hound whispered. "He's taken off again."

Danner wearily pushed to his feet, feeling just too astonished to let his mind full of expletives escape through his lips. "Are Abe and Zed up yet, Hound?"

"Not yet."

"Let them sleep as long as they can."

Because he had no other choices at the time, Danner started rolling up his gear. "Have any idea what time he left?"

Hound was putting the final touches to a rolled cigarette and stuck a match to it before responding. "From the horse turds where his horse was tethered, I'd say sometime in the middle of the night. Tracks leading back south."

"The direction we came from. Imagine that," Danner huffed.

Danner and hound set about rekindling the camp fire and put a skillet of bacon on to fry. The aroma soon aroused the other two, and it took them no time to realize they're party had shrunk in size.

"Yup, boys, Walt Tabor has once again done what Walt Tabor does," Danner started. "Lot of things I could say about that, but I've said them before and they changed not a thing. Truth is, the fight is just not in Walt Tabor. I wish it could be different, but it is what it is, and he is what he is."

Danner took a few seconds to look into the eyes of the others before continuing. "Without him, and what he could have lent to this fight, I wouldn't blame a single one of you if you decided now not to ride with me into Beaver City."

Abe was the first to respond. "I's started out with only two mens who saved my life. Them two mens still here, and I still owes them. If you be ridin', Floyd, Ol' Abe be ridin' with ya."

Danner gave Abe an appreciative smile and a nod of his head.

Hound stepped up close to Danner. "You know what I'll be doing. Nothing more to say on that."

Danner couldn't help but chuckle and slap Hound on the back. He then turned his head to the one man who'd yet to comment. Zed Martin stood upright with his eyes trained on the ground at his feet. After a few seconds he slowly raised his head to look Danner in the eyes.

"Floyd, Hound, Abe…any of you got advice for a man that's never been in a gun fight? I'm damned sure goin' with you, but will heed any words of wisdom on how best to do my part…and stay alive."

Hound and Abe turned their eyes on Danner as well – leaving him the honor to do his job in this matter. "Zed, most importantly, count your rounds. Count them closely. Can't come down to you needing a bullet and you not having one. Next, take your shots at the broadest part of you opponent. Don't matter if it's front parts or rear parts. Dime novels have made back-shooting seem dishonorable.

That's hogwash. You take whatever shot you get to take them down. Finally, seek cover. Standing and delivering without it just makes you a larger and more ignorant target."

Zed nodded his head and grinned. "Do think I can remember that much, Floyd. Many thanks for sharing it."

After breakfast, all set about collecting their gear and readying their horses. Danner was cinching his latigo when Hound strolled up.

"You know, Floyd, I never met CB Wooly or Clay Bardoe," he said in a hushed tone. "I don't talk so much because I concentrate on listening, and I listened closely to all you ever said about them both. So, I feel I know them pretty well by the words you spoke. And know what I think?"

"What do you think, Hound?" Danner grinned.

"I think by the way you've conducted yourself this morning, and the words you've spoken, both CB and Clay would be damned proud of you."

CHAPTER FOURTEEN

That Man

The Apache was cleaning his pistols when Laughing Billy burst through the front doors of the Beaver City Saloon all in a huff, and not emitting any form of laughter.

"Have you been out there, Indian? Seen what's on nearly every damned building up and down the main street?"

Anything that could stop Bemo's laughter certainly demanded the Apache's attention. He stood up from the table where he sat and strode to and out the front door. What had upset Bemo didn't set well with the Apache either. From where he stood, all buildings he could see either bore a sign or had white-washed letters on windows that read the same.

DANNER IS COMING.

Someone clearly intended to arouse the citizenry to have hope and, most likely, incite them to join in the fray upon Danner's arrival.

Thinking out loud, the Apache said, "Had to be the dead storekeeper's wife."

The revelation evidently helped Bemo reinsert his sense of humor. "Yep. Dang sure has to be. She's trouble for sure," Bemo snickered.

The Apache studied Bemo for long seconds before stating, "You have proven to be handy dealing with troublesome women, Laughing Billy. Would you mind paying the dear lady a visit?"

Bemo took off with a determined stride and called back over his shoulder with laughter, "I'll do more than pay her a visit."

* * * *

Margaret Smith forced herself to sit at a desk behind the front counter balancing numbers in a ledger. She did not choose to do the accounting, but wished instead to do yet more to ready the townsfolk for the homecoming of Floyd Danner and whoever might ride in with him. The problem was, she'd talked to all she could talk to, and couldn't think of a way to further the cause. Working on the books only helped to keep her mind productive instead of simply seething over the murdering of her husband.

She'd been careful in her discussions with others not to reveal that her information on Danner had come from Rowland Beans on the insistence of the ousted Marshal Eden Ledford. Awful harm would most certainly befall Beans, Marshal Ledford, and even possibly Mrs. Ledford if the murderers up the street learned of the two men's involvement.

The means of letting all know Danner was on his way had been hung up on signs and painted on windows deep in the night. Margaret was sure the Indian and the madman had by now seen the handiwork she'd instigated among the other business owners. It did startle her, but didn't surprise her, when the door of her shop suddenly flew open with such force that it banged on the opposing wall causing goods to tumble from shelving.

"You have done kicked the wrong dog, woman," Laughing Billy Bemo announced with an evil sounding chuckle.

Margaret jumped up from the desk and tried to make it to the far end of the counter where she kept a pistol. Bemo proved much faster on his feet and brought her to an abrupt halt by grabbing the bun of hair on the top of her head. He used the hold on her hair and a grip of her arm to hoist her up and over the counter. She landed hard enough on the other side of the counter to knock the breath from her lungs. Before she could recover, Bemo had her once again in his grasp.

He jerked her from the floor and shoved her toward the door to her establishment. She tripped and fell, and he grabbed her up again. Bemo shoved and pushed and pulled until she was standing in the middle of the street. Her hair was now loose and tangled and she could feel blood flowing from her nose. Bemo pulled a gun and put it to her head.

"Listen to me all you bastards," he shouted. "Come out behind those doors and windows and start tearing down the signs and rubbing away the white-wash."

"They won't listen to you. They won't do it. We took an oath," Margaret said through gritted teeth.

"They won't?" Bemo cackled. He then shoved Margaret to her knees and put the barrel to the top of her head. "They will after watching this, bitch."

Margaret heard him cock the pistol and she closed her eyes. She knew she would never hear the shot. She started silently praying, but suddenly her silence was broken by a forceful voice.

"BEMO! LET THE WOMAN GO!"

* * * *

Bemo looked in the direction the voice had sounded and saw a lone man sitting a horse on the far south end of the street. Bemo jerked the gun in his hand upward as he pulled another with his free hand. Without careful aim he pulled both triggers and started at a run for the Beaver City Saloon. He watched as the man he couldn't clearly see spurred the horse to a thundering gallop. Since the man came from the south, Bemo figured it could only be the Marshal, Ledford.

Bemo did not make it near far enough before the horse and rider were upon him. Suddenly he felt as if a bolt of lightening struck him low in the back and right above his tail bone, shoving him face down in the dirt. Bemo tried to scramble to his feet, but to his horror, his legs would not obey his demands.

* * * *

Hound was out in the front of the other three and turned in his saddle to holler Danner's name. Danner rode up at a trot.

"See something interesting, Hound?"

Hound nodded thoughtfully and pointed to the ground.

It took Danner a few seconds, but then he spotted them. Horse tracks.

"Tabor's horse," Hound grumbled.

"Tabor? Are you sure?"

"Damned sure, Floyd. He must have just circled the camp to throw us off…He's headed to Beaver City well ahead of us."

Danner pulled in a deep breath, and let it go in a whistle. "I'll be damned," were the only words his suddenly jumbled thinking could produce.

* * * *

By the time Tabor could wheel his horse around, Bemo with a gun in both hands was pulling his body through the dirt street by use of his elbows. At that moment shots were fired from a place north of Tabor. A quick glance revealed the Apache standing in the street in front of the Beaver City Saloon firing from a distance too far away to be accurate with a handgun.

Tabor looked back to Bemo just in time to see him use his hands and arms to flip over onto his back. As Bemo was raising both guns, and laughing like hell, Danner took aim with his pistol.

He fired once.

The top of Bemo's head just turned to mush.

* * * *

Zed and Abe had pulled their horses alongside Danner and Hound, and Danner had tried to explain the inexplicable.

"He's takin' them on by his own damned self?" Zed asked.

"Seems to be the case, Zed," Danner answered.

"And I knows why," Abe replied.

"What are you thinkin', Abe?" Zed asked before Danner could form the question.

"Last night it upset Walt just sumpin' awful seein' what them mens did to Ol' Sawbuck. He didn' wanna see the same happens to any ones of us."

"I'll be damned yet again," Danner replied. "Abe, by God, I think you lassoed the truth just now." Then Danner turned to Hound. "You know this land. If we take off for all these horses can give, how long before we can make Beaver City?"

"All out and out gallop? Maybe an hour and a half, if we don't kill the horses in the process."

Danner bit at his lower lip for a second before making a decision. "Boys, we got to get to Beaver City and Walt. If nothing else, I have some crow to eat. Ride like hell!"

* * * *

The Apache had watched Bemo dragging himself in the dirt, and only one reason a man would do that.

His legs wouldn't work.

He'd also watched the man from near twenty paces on a jittery horse put a bullet in Bemo's head. Not just any man could do that with a handgun. With only two shots fired, the man had destroyed Laughing Billy Bemo.

The Apache took a few steps further into the street, staring at the man on the horse, who simply sat calmly staring back. The only thing he could tell about the man from this distance, was like himself, the man was no shabby dresser. No cowhand.

The Apache took a few steps further into the street and started reloading his pistols as he shouted.

"What is your name?"

The man called his name loud and clear, and the Apache had not mistaken it.

"I've been told you are not a courageous man," the Apache shouted.

"That's putting it kindly," the man shouted back.

"Do you now feel courageous enough to take on a man who can't be killed?"

"Oh, you can be killed…by the right man…I'm *that man*."

The Apache had holstered his weapons during the exchange. He now pulled them again and held them down at his side. "Ready when you are, Walt Tabor!"

* * * *

Tabor reloaded the revolver he'd used to kill Bemo. Once that was done, he kept it in his right hand, and removed the other with his left hand. He let the horse have his reigns and put the spurs to his flanks. He was still about one-hundred yards from his target when the Apache started to fire. It would take a lucky shot to hit a man on a fast-moving horse at that distance. Tabor held his fire.

At fifty yards, one of the Apache's rounds went through Tabor's coat only singeing his flesh – a glancing blow. The Apache had now fired all rounds from the revolver in his right hand. He dropped it to the ground and transferred the pistol in his left hand to his right. Danner took careful aim with the pistol in his right hand. He cocked the hammer and pulled the trigger.

* * * *

Margaret Smith had not bothered pushing to her feet, but still remained on her knees in the street – mesmerized and held immobile by the violence that played out right before her eyes. She'd had a bird's eye view of the destruction of Billy Bemo. She clearly saw the shot taken that immobilized his legs and distinctly heard him cry out in pain before pulling himself forward like a slithering snake. She heard his laugher as he flopped over on his back and she let out a faint cry of relief when the second bullet tore asunder the top of his head.

She did not immediately recognize the extraordinarily dressed man on the horse, but knew he looked familiar. She could not call his name until he answered the Apache's question.

"My name is Walt Tabor!"

Now she watched as Tabor barreled down on the Apache on his charging horse. She saw the Apache switch guns and Walt Tabor taking aim. The first shot he fired struck the Apache high on the left side of his body, spun him in place, and put him down but sitting upright on his ass.

The Apache raised the gun in his right hand and did for the first time put effort in his aiming. The shot he fired found it's mark and the front legs of Tabor's horse folded beneath its body. Tabor flew over the lowered head and shoulders of his horse, hitting the ground hard – helpless to do anything but tumble. The revolvers in his hands came loose, and when Tabor finally rolled to a stop, he scrambled to regain them.

The Apache had managed to push to his feet and hobbled toward Tabor, firing his pistol as he advanced. By Tabor's bodily movements Margaret could tell at least two of the bullets found their mark.

The Apache was nearly upon Tabor before the downed gunmen laid hands on one of his revolvers and got off a quick but accurate shot.

* * * *

Maybe he only imagined he saw the bullet exit the barrel. Most likely just the working of a brain giving up its soul, but it seemed he watched the path of the bullet lead straight to the near center of his chest.

It stopped the Apache in his tracks. His right hand relaxed and the gun it held fell to the street. He lowered his head and watched the blood as it gushed from a hole that certainly led to his heart. The Apache began to wobble on his feet. He only had moments to study Tabor, lying on his back, his head brought forward, his eyes staring.

"Walt Tabor," the Apache said as he began to choke on his own blood, "You are *that man.*"

* * * *

Tabor slowly laid his head back to rest on the ground and closed his eyes. He didn't know how many times he'd been hit, but instinctively knew he would not survive his wounds. He didn't know how long he laid on the ground, doing his best just to pull air into his lungs, before someone knelt beside him and took his hand.

"You were so very brave," a female voice said softly. "You saved our town, Deputy Tabor."

It seemed it took all the strength he had to just open his eyes. It took him long moments, but he did finally recognize the face of Margaret Smith.

The woman CB Wooly loved…and could never have.

His thoughts turned immediately to the love he would now never know, and he felt his eyes filling with a mist. He started seeing other forms gathering and looking down upon him – offering words of admiration and appreciation.

"Help me," Margaret Smith said, "we must get him to the doctor."

"No," Tabor pleaded, "Don't move me. Danner is coming. Just please help me stay alive until his arrival."

Margaret told someone to fetch the doctor. Tabor knew his coming would make no difference in the outcome. He could feel the blood draining from his body.

Margaret patted the hand she held. Someone applied pressure to his abdomen. For a moment he mistook Margaret for Annie Francis. He tried to raise a hand to touch her face, but he only got it inches off the ground before it fell back in place.

For an amount of time he could not account for, he went back – to his mother's side – to the hills he'd roamed as a teen – to the time he spent at the side of CB Wooly. He stood with Annie, holding her hand. Sharing love and laughter and making plans for their future.

And after, maybe, a great length of time he heard the words he'd hung on to hear.

Danner is coming!

* * * *

"Walt, it's me, Floyd."

Danner watched as Tabor struggled to open his eyes. Danner sensed that when he again closed them, they would forever be shut. Zeb, Abe, and Hound had pushed back the crowd, and now they, like Danner, knelt on bended knee around their fallen friend.

"Guess this was the day I should have ran, boys," Tabor said with a slight smile.

"It was a great thing you did here today, Walt. I could not have done the same," Danner said.

Tabor pulled in several shallow breaths before attempting to speak again. "Man reaps what he sows. The Apache and Bemo are now reaping hellfire. Stu Graybow needs to do the same. Don't think I'll be able to help you with that, Floyd."

"You've certainly done your part, Walt. I will do my damndest to do mine."

Tabor began to tremble as if cold. "Floyd, tell Annie…tell her I loved her, and that my last thoughts were of her."

Before Danner could respond, Tabor closed his eyes and grew still. Moments later he exhaled his last breath.

CHAPTER FIFTEEN

No Further Obligation

Danner and his men pushed to their feet. Looking down into the now relaxed face of Walt Tabor, Danner could not put terms to his feelings. They were like an impotent sky of dark and foreboding clouds that rumbled and roared but produced no storm. He did know for sure that he now wished he'd been kinder to Tabor the past days they'd been together.

Danner knew what his men needed now was something to take their minds off the body lying at their feet.

"Hound, will you find the undertaker? Tell him we'll be taking Walt back with us when we leave for Texas?

"Sure thing, boss," Hound said before stepping off to complete his task.

"Abe and Zed, we'll need fresh horses. You two mind dealing with the livery man?"

"Don' minds a' all," Abe answered.

"Be glad to, Floyd," Zed nodded.

Danner knew his men needed rest. He decided to seek lodging. He turned and nearly bumped into a woman with blood drying on her upper lip and her face showing signs of swelling and bruising. It took him a second to recognize the woman as Mrs. Smith, the store keeper's wife.

"Who did you this harm, Mrs. Smith?"

"The laughing moron. He would have killed me had not Deputy Tabor intervened."

Words were not coming easily for Danner, so he just nodded his head.

"Believe me, Deputy Danner, he was an angel sent by God. Those two murdering scoundrels have wreaked havoc since entering our town. First, they banished the city marshal to stand guard outside of town. I assume you met him. Don't know why he didn't ride in with either Deputy Tabor or you and your men. Maybe he's now tending to his wife, bless their hearts."

Danner knew the answer to her question, and knew the marshal was not now or would never again tend to the needs of his wife. They'd found the body wearing a badge. Danner decided he just didn't care at the moment to share that with a woman who'd witnessed enough death for one day.

"After that, they killed my husband and town mayor. They shot poor…"

"Killed your husband?" Danner interrupted. "Mrs. Smith, I'm so very sorry for your loss."

"They also shot an older man that showed up for reasons I'm not aware of, but do know the same man just minutes earlier shot and killed two of the men that Stu Graybow road in with and…"

"Stu Graybow? He's here?" Danner interrupted again, this time with a quickened beat of his heart.

"Not here now. Would imagine he's at his ranch."

"How long ago was this, Mrs. Smith? How many men did he have with him?"

"My days are kind of jumbled, Deputy Danner. Guessing maybe two days at the most. Can't forget how many men he had with him, they being such a cut-throat looking gang. There were five, but the big old man killed two. Three rode out with Graybow."

Danner thanked Margaret Smith for the invaluable information and once again offered condolences. He started to walk away, but was assaulted by another thought.

"Mrs. Smith, did you see the gun battle here today?"

"See it? I was practically right in the middle of it, sir."

Danner drew in a deep breath before asking, "Would you mind terribly telling me how it all happened?"

* * * *

Rowland Beans was more than happy to provide rooms for Danner and his men, and refused profusely any exchange of money. Danner gathered his men after the competing of their assigned tasks and now they all stood at the bar of the Beaver City Saloon.

Danner told them about his conversation with Mrs. Smith, starting with the way Walt Tabor had gloriously bested the Apache and Laughing Billy. He ended by sharing the news of Stu Graybow and his hired hands.

"Damn, that makes it easy for us," Zed responded to the news.

"Does it, Zed?" Danner asked. "I mean, I do understand that this means we no longer have to track them down, but the way I see it, we only got two choices. Do we go to the ranch, or do we get them to come here?"

"How would we get them to come here?" Hound asked.

"Don't know, Hound, and maybe that's not the best play. I just know it's now four against four, thanks to Sawbuck Sam, but three of their four are hired gun hands. I'm betting that anyone of those three in a fair fight could take any one of us four. I've lost one…Not willing to lose another. That's the reason I'll now ask for any advice or ideas you men might have."

Abe offered the first response, "Goin' back to my army days, I mights have an idea how's best to skin this cat, Floyd."

Danner, Hound, and Zed listened to Abe's suggestion. Questions were asked, and Abe provided sound answers. After only minutes more of discussion, Danner made his decision.

"I like it, Abe. I like it a hell of a lot."

Zed and Hound agreed.

"Only thing on this plan that comes to mind," Danner said, "is that this is not a way of doing business that Walt Tabor would have agreed with."

Surprisingly, Hound responded quickly with a rebuttal. "Don't know how else to put this, and don't mean to sound unkind, Floyd, but…Walt's dead."

* * * *

The sun was just saying hello to a new day when Tim Swonger stepped out onto the grand porch with a steaming cup of coffee. He placed the cup on the railing and began the process of rolling his first cigarette of the morning. His mind fell to thinking about the poor night of sleep he'd gotten because of the going-ons of young Friday and the Madam Henry. He had enjoyed old man Graybow's ire over the arrangement, and could only hope he could hear as much from his room that Swonger could from his. The old man's insistence on being called, "Mr. Graybow," rubbed Swonger the wrong way. His arrogance needed the whittling down the Kid provided.

Swonger put the freshly rolled cigarette to his lips and lit it. He pulled smoke deep into his lungs, even before he could push it back out, all faded to black.

* * * *

Jack Friday sprung from the bed at the sound of a single gunshot.

"Stay with me, Jack. Don't go out there," Martha pleaded.

"Can't do that," Friday responded as he hurriedly got into his clothes and grabbed up his gun belt.

He nearly ran right into Graybow on the second-floor landing. The old man held a revolver in each hand.

"Where did the shot come from?" Graybow huffed.

"Have no idea," Friday responded as he bound down the stairs in front of Graybow.

Pink Corning called from somewhere down stairs, "Swonger is dead. Check the windows on all sides of the house. We need to know how many is out there."

"You sure he's dead?" Graybow called.

"Pretty sure. Half his head is gone," Corning replied and then added, "Think whoever fired the shot is behind that huge cottonwood out front."

Friday started going from window to window. It proved to be an easy and safe task since the house had been built when the Comanche were still a threat and all down stair windows had interior shudders with peep holes. Peering through the fourth window produced possible results.

"Pink! Thought I saw movement in the upper north window of the barn."

"Got one on the backside too," Graybow shouted. "Just saw a head poke out from behind the outhouse."

The three men converged in the dining room at the center of the large house. "Pretty sure they have us surrounded," Corning said. "I'm going to watch the big tree out front. Kid, you watch that barn window, and Graybow you stake yourself out on the outhouse."

Friday didn't mind taking orders from Corning, but was not surprised when Graybow bristled.

"Nothing's changed around here on who gives the orders, Corning, or on the proper calling of my name."

Corning moved up close to Graybow. "Okay, *Mr. Graybow,* how do you want it done?"

"I want Friday to advance on the barn. Chances are he just saw one of the Joiner family in that window."

"Too big a chance to take, *Mr. Graybow.* We don't know how many are out there. Here, under cover, we might be able to take a few out, try to pull out any others that are out there."

Corning turned back to Friday. "Grab your Winchester, Kid, put some bullets through and around that window in the barn. Boss man there can do whatever he think's best." Corning already had his rifle and now moved out for the front part of the house.

Friday knelt before the window opposite the barn and didn't even have the shutter open before Corning opened fire from his position.

"By God there was one behind that giant tree," he hollered, "but not no more. Got him!"

Friday pumped six shots to the left and right of the barn window, knowing his rounds had a good chance of penetrating the planked wood. If he did any good, he saw no signs of doing so. He was closing the shutter to move to another window when a voice called out from around and maybe inside the barn.

"Listen up in the house! You have five minutes before we set it a' fire. You have that much time to come out with your hands empty and showing." The voice reverberated with anger. Whoever it belonged to no doubt took great objection to one of his crew taking a bullet from Corning.

Friday ran to find Corning, who was looking out another window. "Spotted anymore?" he asked.

"No."

"Pink, I'm thinking this might be a good time to try and make it to the barn and our horses."

Corning looked Friday in the eyes and nodded, "I have no better idea."

* * * *

Graybow heard the conversation between Corning and Friday, and didn't care to try and stop them. Instead he made his way upstairs and to Martha Henry's room. She stood dressed, hurriedly placing items in a bag.

"I came to tell you to do just that," Graybow said.

"I heard the man," she said without looking up from her packing.

Graybow watched her preparing to leave without feeling any remorse. Her stunt of taking in the younger man had turned Graybow's heart cold against her.

What are you going to do?" she asked over her shoulder.

"I'm not leaving my house."

Graybow wasn't convinced they'd actually burn him down. Even if they did, going up in flames seemed a better alternative than hanging. He was turning to leave when he heard a door open downstairs and a voice shout out a plea.

"Don't shoot! Please don't shoot! I'm a writer, not a combatant!"

"Cowardly son of a bitch," Graybow grumbled as he quickly started making his way downstairs.

"You can come out with your hands in the air," the voice from outside shouted. "Make your way to the outbuildings on the west side of the house."

Graybow made it downstairs just in time to see Corning and Friday pile in behind Hathcoat, placing guns to his back. Both could practically fit behind his broad torso. They shoved him out the door and turned him in the direction of the big barn on the east side of the house.

* * * *

It surprised Friday that they made it halfway between the house and the barn without encountering any of the men or being shot at. They made it a few more steps before Hathcoat simply gave all he had to give. When his knees buckled and he went down, Friday knew it was no ploy, but just out and out fear. The smell of shit in his trousers couldn't be mistaken.

The moment Hathcoat went down, two men popped into the large doorway to the barn with a rifle and a mighty fancy shotgun at the ready. Corning managed to get off one round. He took down the man with the rifle, but then the shotgun opened up, practically ripping Corning in half.

Friday raised his rifle to his shoulder, but that's as far as he got before it felt like a mule kicked him in the back of that shoulder. The impact of the round spun Friday in place and his rifle went flying. He grabbed for his revolver, but before he could clear it from its leather, the barrel of the fancy shotgun loomed inches from his face.

"You don's has to die young 'un."

Friday had so concentrated on the new kind of shotgun that he'd failed to even notice the man's skin color until he looked him in the face.

"I'd rather die here than be hauled off to hang," Friday said.

A voice called out from behind Friday. "We ain't the law, and we don't intend to kill you unless you give us no other choice."

Friday removed his hand from the grips of his Colt.

"Hurry and grab him, Abe," the voice called again. "Get to cover. Graybow's still standing."

* * * *

Danner had fired the shot, that took the young man down, from behind the ancient cotton wood tree and while standing over the body at his feet. As fate would have it, this man, and the one just gunned down in the doorway of the barn were the only two he could recruit from Beaver City to ride on Graybow and his gunmen. The two men, Les Bonds and Jody Piles had sometimes served as deputies for Marshal Ledford and took great offense at him being dead. Danner had not been able to prove it, but told them and the other men from town that he highly suspected it had been Graybow's men who murdered the marshal. The other men from town had good enough reasons for not joining up with Danner – families, lack of experience with firearms and the such.

"Abe!" Danner called out. "How bad off is Piles?"

"He's wid da angels, Floyd," Abe shouted back.

Danner ducked his head and shook it, he truly hated talking two brave men into dying. He immediately chased off and chastised the thought that rebutted his emotions – *better these two than one of my three.* He promised himself to see that Piles and Bonds got funerals befitting the heroes they were.

Danner had been so deep in his thoughts and grief that he didn't notice the woman until she was well in out in the front yard. They were close enough he thought she looked familiar, but couldn't put a place or name to the face.

"Lady! Get over here behind this tree or over there inside the barn," he ordered.

The woman chose to join Danner behind the cottonwood. She was only feet away when Danner recognized her.

"I don't recall your name, but will be damned if you don't show a knack for being where men die. You were in Stillwater the day CB Wooly killed Clay Bardoe."

The woman glared at Danner and said with guile, "If you don't know who I am, then you have no need of knowing at this point."

Danner simply shrugged his shoulders and raised a cupped palm to the side of his mouth. "Hound? Zed? Can you hear me?"

"I can hear you, Floyd," Hound shouted back.

"Me too, Floyd," Zed returned.

"Set the house on fire, boys!"

* * * *

Graybow heard the order being issued. He paused for only a second to look around his beloved home, and bitterness over its impending destruction overtook him. Graybow reached into his pocket and pulled out a trophy he'd carried since the day he'd taken it. Pinning the star, with a hole through it, to his lapel seemed an appropriate way to placate his anguish. Graybow then quickly started moving from window to window in hopes of spotting the direction from which one or both of the men would travel to set his house on fire. He held in his hands a double-barreled shotgun with both hammers cocked. If he got lucky enough to spot either man, he'd send them to hell with a gaping hole through their midsection.

Finally, his luck changed, and he spotted one running up on the east side of his house with a lit lantern in hand. Suddenly other men started pumping rounds at the house. The man with the lantern gave it a sling, and Graybow let go with both barrels. The lantern collided with the house and Graybow heard the resulting explosion. Then he heard the same on the far side of the house. Still, Graybow let out a laugh. The first man, catching the full force of both Graybow's barrels in the chest would cause no more damage on this day or any other.

* * * *

Danner fired his Winchester at the house until it was empty. By then, the grand structure was magnificently on fire. Danner placed his back against the towering and broad tree and started reloading his rifle. If Graybow chose to exit the front door, Danner did not intend for him to make it far. In the meeting the night before, all had agreed that if it came down to the house being set on fire, Graybow would not leave the ranch alive. If, he came out, begging for his life, Danner now decided, at the very least he would hang from the tree that now provided Danner cover and concealment.

Evidently not caring for his company, the woman left the tree and headed at a nonchalant pace toward the barn. Little of the house now stood that wasn't consumed by the flames, and just moments later, Danner heard screams coming from the inside. He set his eyes upon the woman to see how she reacted to the displayed anguish. She didn't – just kept on walking. Evidently, Graybow meant nothing to her.

Danner didn't have to wait long before the front door flew open, and Graybow stumbled through the doorway and onto the long porch. The hair on his head and his beard were singed away. His arms, shoulders, and back were ablaze. He flayed his arms trying to use his hands to extinguish the flames. Utter anguish was apparent by the expression on his face and the screams he emitted through charred lips. He clearly and prematurely endured already the fires of hell.

"Put me out of my misery!" he cried out.

Danner raised the Winchester and took aim.

As CB Wooly struggled with his last breaths on earth…Stu Graybow put yet another bullet through his badge and heart."

The thought burned in Danner's mind with nearly the same intensity as the actual flames did in devouring the flesh of an evil man who deserved no quarter. Danner slowly lowered his rifle and stepped away from the tree. He did not take his eyes off Graybow until he finally fell from the porch and onto the ground. Only when the kicking and thrashing dwindled to mere twitching did Danner turn from Graybow to walk toward the big barn.

✱ ✱ ✱ ✱

Zed Martin walked up to the big barn as Floyd and Abe worked to lay the two friends, Bonds and Piles, side by side. An older woman stood by watching with a most curious look on her face. A younger man, not much more than a kid, was seated, leaning against the barn, and cradling his bloody right shoulder with his left hand. A rather fat man in banker style clothing sat next to him breathing heavily. Floyd looked up at Zed as he approached.

"Where's Hound, Zed?"

Zed had made the trek around the burning house feeling as if his feet weighed more than his body, and his heart weighed more than his feet. He spoke his tormented thoughts out loud.

"You don't know."

"What do you mean, Zed?" Floyd asked.

"You and Abe best come with me," Zed replied as he turned and pulled forth all the strength he could muster to walk back to where he'd been.

Floyd and Abe followed without comment, but when they made the last corner of what remained of the big house, and what needed to be seen could be seen, both Floyd and Abe passed Zed in a run. Floyd collapsed to his knees next to the body, and Abe placed a hand on Floyd's shoulder. Zed continued his plodding pace until he stood next to Abe.

Floyd, on his knees with his head hanging low, took quick and sniffling breaths while he wiped at eyes that Zed thankfully could not see. Zed sensed that Abe, like himself, felt obliged to remain silent until Floyd decided to break the silence. After long and agonizing moments, Floyd pushed to his feet. Zed continued to avoid looking him in the eyes.

"Thought I'd made it through this awful ordeal with all my friends still standing," Floyd said in a voice that cracked with emotion.

"Floyd, theys be a buckboard in da barn," Abe said softly. "You wants me to load Hound into it?"

Floyd stood silently for seconds before turning moist and bloodshot eyes on Zed. "Tell me if I'm wrong, Zed, but I'm thinking a cowboy like Hound would prefer taking his last ride strapped over a fine horse like ol' Moonshine."

Zed nodded his head. "Think you'd be right, Floyd."

"Thanks, Zed. Abe, please do rig the buckboard. I'd prefer it for delivering Walt back to Annie."

Zed stood in place as Abe took off for the barn. In times when nothing really needed to be said, Zed felt a need to say something. "Floyd, what are we going to do with that woman and the two fellers?"

"Not our responsibility, Zed. We'll leave them to do what every they will do."

"What about Graybow? We going to bury him?"

"You once worked for the man. Unless you feel otherwise, we'll let those three do the burying that needs done. If they choose not to bury him, I say let the buzzards and coyote have what remains of the man who murdered CB Wooly."

Zed searched his conscious and said, "I'd grown close to Hound Olivo. As for the man who killed him, I feel no further obligation than to let him rot."

CHAPTER SIXTEEN

Fit Him Well

It'd been a very long and complexing day of bouncing in the buckboard's seat, and Danner didn't think he had a muscle not reminding him of the full day of travel. It'd been a lonely day as well. One in which Danner could not help but fall victim to his tormenting thoughts. However, he'd expected as much and prepared for it as well. Before leaving Beaver City he'd bought the finest bottle of whiskey that Roland Beans had on hand.

Earlier that morning, after the undertaker and assistants had loaded Tabor's coffin in the buckboard, Abe and Zed approached Danner on horseback. He could tell by the way they dismounted that they were bearing a troublesome load.

"Floyd, you got a minute," Zed asked with a grimace.

"Yup. Just waiting on you two. I'm ready to head south when you are,"

"Well, on that very thing, we'd like to tell you what we're thinking. Now, Floyd, if you don't agree, we won't do it."

Danner pulled in a deep breath. "Do what, Zed?"

"Well, Abe, here, has asked me to go in with him on his farming idea, and maybe doing a little ranching as well. I told him I'd be pleased as a dog eating shit to do just that. Well, we ain't in no great hurry, but are anxious to get to looking for the right land, and we got to thinking…"

"Got to thinking you'd just ride east from here?" Danner said, forcing a smile.

"Well, I mean, neither of us would up and just leave you high and dry if it meant all that much for us to accompany you and the ladies to Claude, Texas, but that's about five days…"

"Boys, I think it's a splendid idea," Floyd lied. "Hell, no need in you going that far out of your way. I'm sure the twins would surely understand, and ol' Walt Tabor would as well."

It was not pleasing news for Danner, but he did fully understand. It wasn't that he particularly needed the two on the trip. It simply came down to the fact that he wasn't just yet ready to part ways with either of them.

"Now's yo sho about dis, Floyd. You knows how's much I be owin' yous."

"Oh, hell's bells, Abe, you done paid me twice over anything I ever owed you. What you two have in front of you is important, and I think it best you get right to it."

Had the two been the selfish type, they could have left the day before, but had stuck around to help Danner endure the burying of Hound Olivo. Danner's manner of saying good-bye to Abe and Zed, for a man not comfortable in doing so, was a simple shaking of hands and promising to one day see each other again. Danner knew the chances of doing so were slim.

Now, as he sat beside his campfire chugging from his bottle of whiskey, he missed them both, and he missed Hound, and a part of him he didn't care to poke – missed Walt Tabor as well. To tell the truth, that's why he'd bought the whiskey right after Zed and Abe rode away. Danner had known the loneliest part of his journey would be the one night spent beside the road. He'd also known the idle period before finding sleep would be the most likely time to confront what tormented him so.

Did I do the right thing at Graybow's ranch?

Oh, he knew the answer the man would give whose body now lay in a coffin not ten feet away. On such, he held the bottle now that was nearly half consumed toward the wagon in a salute.

"Appreciate what you did and how you did it, but not listening to your crap tonight, Walt."

All had agreed on the decisions made the night before the raid on the ranch. They'd agreed to simply shoot down any man they initially encountered to reduce Graybow's numbers and increase their own odds. Had they come upon all of them in the open, they would have opened fire on all of them. Any chance given to surrender to those type of men, all had agreed, would have just given them the chance to get off the first shots fired. Finally, on Graybow, all gave a nod on the fact he would not leave his ranch alive, and no way could be too awful of a way for him to die.

Danner took a very mighty slug of the whiskey. "Not listening to you, Walt."

It was all out and out murder.

"The hell it was," Danner slightly slurred his words. "It was self-defense, by God!"

It was a massacre.

Danner struggled to get to his feet, and then faced off with the wagon bearing the coffin. "That is utter bullshit! We did not kill the woman, or the writer, or the kid, for that matter. Now, that would have been murder and a massacre, and a crying shame to put."

Go ahead and ask the question that burns in your soul.

"Won't do it. Don't have to because he wasn't there."

It was the very question Danner had chased from his thinking since the night they made the plans on the raid. He'd not even let it form as a complete sentence in his mind. Still it occurred to him several times, as it did now, that it would have been a question Walt Tabor would have confronted him with.

WOULD HE HAVE DONE THE SAME THING?

Swaying on his feet, Danner brought the bottle to his lips and downed what remained of its contents. He then threw the bottle at the wagon, and missed. Turning from the wagon, he plopped down hard on his ass. It was all gone. The whiskey that is. The question still burned and if not confronted, Danner so feared it would have a sobering effect.

"Would CB Wooly have done what I did?" he said in barely a whisper.

Danner pulled from his memory every encounter with the man. Tried his hardest to remember every single conversation, and the answer came in a rush.

"Had all things been the same, which they would have been, then, by God, CB would have done the same or, at least, something similar.

Damn right he would have.

Floyd Danner stretched out on the ground next to the fire and mumbled his last words on the matter.

"Good night, Walt."

* * * *

Guessing it too gorgeous of a day to be trapped inside the cabin, Danner could see the four women sitting in the front yard. Moments later, they spotted him as well. When he figured to be at a recognizable distance, two of the women came to their feet and started in a run toward him. From the great span that separated them, Danner could not tell Fannie from Annie, until one suddenly came to a dead stop. He knew it must be Annie, and she had to be wondering why he was alone on a wagon pulling two rider-less horses behind him. He also noted a way in which Fannie had changed her pace. Instead of a romping run, she now ran with determination as if to find out what had gone wrong. She too came to a stop about forty paces from the wagon and brought her hands up to cover her mouth. From that distance she'd no doubt spotted the coffin in the back of the buckboard. Annie had turned and started plodding back to the cabin.

Danner pulled the reigns to stop the wagon alongside Fannie. He'd thought he would jump down and grab her into his arms, but how drastically the glee had turned to gloom held him in place. Fannie's eyes were trained on the two horses tied behind the wagon. One was Floyd's and the other was Moonshine.

"That's Hound in the box?" her voice trembled.

She'd not known instinctively what sent Annie back and into the cabin.

"No, Fannie. It's Walt."

Tears started to spill from her eyes. "All are gone?" she gasped.

"Not all. Just Hound and Walt. Zed and Abe went on their way. We buried Hound in Beaver City."

Fannie lowered her head into her hands and began to sob. Danner sat the brake and crawled down from the wagon to take Fannie gently into his arms.

"I thought it best to take Walt on to Claude with us," he said softly as he felt her trembling in his grasp.

"Poor, poor Annie," Fannie shuttered. Several minutes passed before she spoke again. "I cry not only for Hound, and Walt, and for my sister, but cry also out of relief that you returned back to me."

Danner gave her a slight squeeze. "I told you all along that I'd be back."

Fannie pulled her head from his shoulder and looked into his eyes. "What will you do in Claude?"

"You mean besides being a husband and having a passel of children?"

"Besides that," she smiled faintly.

"Well, what would you want me to do?"

Fannie pulled to the extended length of his arms and reached to hold his face in both of hers. "I just hope you do not desire to wear a badge."

Floyd smiled down at her. "I've worn a badge, and think I wore it long enough. No, I've been thinking, if you'd allow it, I'd just help you and Annie out with the store you've inherited from your aunt."

Fannie's expression turned hopeful. "You truly think you'd be satisfied with such a mundane existence?"

Danner again pulled Fannie in close and looked over her shoulder at the rough and rugged terrain. As far as he could see was land that white men had wrestled away from the Comanche at a tremendous cost of blood and death – a land where most men now either rode with a badge, or rode to get away from one.

"Honestly, Fannie, after all I've seen and done the past few days, mundane seems downright welcoming. Besides, once knew a man of my ilk that became a storekeeper. Seemed to fit Clay Bardoe just fine. Reckon it will do the same for me."

ACKNOWLEDGMENTS

To Henry P. Scully of Scully Associates. Pat, many thanks for another eye-catching cover design.

To David Shupe for line and story editing. David, thanks for finding so many mistakes and making suggestions that improved this story.

To Sohail Liaqat for formatting and technical support with the manuscript. Sohail, thanks for taking so much time and effort in getting this book ready for publication.

To Steve Allen for use of his property. Steve, thanks for letting us use the structures on your property for the book cover.

ABOUT THE AUTHOR

Keith Remer is a retired Army colonel. After thirty-two years of service in the Army, he taught various courses as an adjunct professor before buying a horse ranch. He has to date written twelve novels and is the recipient of the *International Indy Book Award for Best in Fiction* for his thriller, *The Hiding Place of Thunder*. Keith lives on his horse ranch in rural Oklahoma City where he writes his novels and tends his horses.

To connect with Keith, visit his Facebook page @KeithRemerAuthor, or his webpage: keithremer.com